When Adam Lacroft Met Death

Carlos Paolini

 **New Generation Publishing**

The Day I Studied For Math

I guess we can start things off with how perfect my life was—was—right up until it ended. And I don't mean metaphorically: I literally passed on to establish an "it's complicated" relationship with Death (the crazy bitch made a pass at me) and that pretty much screwed everything up. Seriously, out of all the women I've... you know what? We'll get to that.

One would have to discuss what it is I define as perfect, so let me rephrase that—my concept of perfect, which overall made me happy. A teenage life in which three needs coexisted beautifully: decent grades, physical necessities and entertainment. I considered decent grades a necessity because, once I finished school, they were the one thing that would have made it possible for me to have the other two. That's how it works—decent grades, you get a decent job and after that you can always marry someone rich. Physical necessities are pretty obvious; they're the things you absolutely need to carry on with your life like food, water, health insurance and membership at the nearest gigamarket or gym, or both if possible. And my favorite, entertainment. Entertainment covers movies, books and girls. TV used to be in there but its quality started declining after the early 2000s and I gave up hope after a certain reality show that was about ten idiots living in a house by the beach.

That's it.

No prize, no eliminations.

Just ten idiots living in a house by the shore.

Movies were usually the means to an end, which was generally a girl, but I still watched a lot of them. Books proved to be very helpful with assignments, teachers, parents and their lovely daughters. That leads me to the last aspect of my entertainment needs, girls. Girls need no explanation.

So when I was still alive, a Thursday, I was living by this creed. I woke up tired, but studying late hadn't really helped me out. Somehow I actually felt less informed for my test on Friday. I got off the bed and picked up my phone to see what time it was: "7:15, Thursday, October 17." I had to change fast, Mr. Connor was giving a special class in first period to prepare idiots like me for the exam and I couldn't afford to miss a single minute. As I was putting on the first T-shirt I found in my closet my phone gave out a high-pitched scream. It was a text from Erica: "Bring my math notebook dumbass, I swear if you forget I'll...." I put my phone in my pocket. I had totally forgotten she lent me her notebook.

Erica was... Erica was everything to me. We met when we were kids. I was seven years old and I was fooling around on the swings in a park when this little red-haired girl holding an ice cream cone came up to me: "You know you shouldn't be playing around like that, it's dangerous."

I jumped off the swing. "Well didn't you know?" I glared at her. "Danger is my middle name." Even today I have no idea where that came from—probably something I saw in a movie—but I'm proud to say I've been cool for as long I can remember. Okay, it was a somewhat aggressive response coming from a seven-year-old, but then again, where did she get off telling me how to play in my playground?

"Oh yeah?" She licked the strawberry ice cream. "Well, I heard your middle name was Stupid." She licked the ice cream again, not even bothering to look at my reaction.

I walked closer to her and slapped the ice cream cone out of her hand. Then I stood, just watching. She started slowly collapsing: a huge frown drew across her face, her eyes started watering and she let go a sob. I walked closer and stepped on the remains of the ice cream.

She ran to her mom, crying.

I didn't see her again until two weeks later when we started at ClearValley Elementary School. I bullied Erica a lot the first month, reminding her of our first encounter mainly by knocking something out of her hands. At least twice a day I sent her desserts, notebooks, pencil cases, etc. flying.

But one day she got me back. She put superglue on the cover of one of her notebooks and walked past me on purpose, knowing I'd fall for it. Then she told one of the teachers and since the evidence was stuck to my hand I finally got busted. However, since she had chemically bonded her grammar notebook to my hand on purpose we both got punished and had to stay after school for a week, cleaning the desks. In that week we came to a truce and we have been best friends ever since, although she still sometimes claimed that I had emotionally scarred her for life.

By that Thursday morning though, and for some time before it, this was no longer the kind of relationship I wanted with her. For one thing, she was insanely hot. Her bright ginger hair had turned darker throughout the years and now it was almost brown, but with flashes of red when the sun hit it. Her eyes went from deep blue to a color I have trouble describing, like sea-green, but the edges perfectly marked in black. She was an average height, but the rest of her body was flawless: curves well marked, perfect abdomen. I'm pretty sure Mrs. God wasn't around when God made Erica. But putting aside her paranormal attractiveness, she was the most important girl in my life and we had spent so much time together we could read each other's mind. I'm not sure as to why we weren't together as a couple. It's not that she was out of my league, please, as if I ever had a league limitation. It's not that we saw each other as brother and sister. I think it was mainly because she knew I hadn't had a relationship that had lasted more than two months. Or maybe she just liked messing with me. Erica knew I loved her and I knew she loved me.

I grabbed Erica's notebook, ate a quick bowl of cereal and left for school. I arrived with a few minutes to spare. Erica was already there, lying down in the hall outside Mr. Connor's classroom, eyes closed, using her backpack as a pillow.

"Come on Erica, really? Do you know how many people walk across this floor?"

She gave a faint groan without opening her eyes. "Do you?"

"A lot." I sighed. *"Anda, mi cielo, parate que se ve feo."*

That made her open her eyes. "Come on, that's not fair! You know I'm helpless against your Spanish." She sat up, laughing.

"I'm sorry, you left me no choice."

Spanish was one of my best cards. It worked like a charm on American girls and even better on Latin ones. My aunt lives in Venezuela and she's a great teacher. I had spent four summers in her house there so I spoke Spanish fluently. *"Mi cielo"* means literally "my sky." I picked that up from her husband, and sometimes my dad said it too. In South America couples use it a lot, it's like how American couples call each other "honey" or "sweetheart," so that's what I called Erica sometimes. I leaned over and helped her get up just as the bell rang.

"Let's do this," I said, summoning the courage to try

to understand something in the upcoming hours of useless combinations of numbers, shapes, angles and Greek letters.

"Yeah, my hopes aren't that high either."

That was a lie. Well, more like a delusion. Maybe her hopes weren't that high, but she had no trouble with math. Erica had this habit of believing she was worse at something than she actually was.

"Not this bullshit again. Last time you said that, what grade did you get?"

"An A minus"

"I'm sorry, could you say that a little louder?"

"AN A MINUS, you made your point, asshole."

"A fucking A minus, of course I made my point."

She laughed at my aggressiveness. We always talked like that, but we rarely offended each other.

"Gosh, sorry. I still get nervous, you know?" she said as we walked into the classroom.

I took my seat and stared at the board. Mr. Connor had already drawn a perfect isosceles triangle, with a square on one of the edges identifying the right angle, and the length of one of the sides shown. Simple enough. Through one of the two functions I knew I got the angle of that side and managed to solve the problem. I wrote down the different lengths for each side and, with a little trouble, got through two other exercises. I was proud of my progress and I thought that maybe this test wasn't going to be impossible. I looked at the clock and fifteen minutes had passed since the class started, only one hour and fifteen to go. But then, like always, Mr. Connor pulled out the big guns. He started drawing circles with triangles in them and then squares with imaginary and real triangles in them and then trapezoids with triangles and random striped zones in them, asking for like three different numbers from each group of figures. I copied all the necessary info on them but left the figures like that. I would ask Erica to help me out later or, worst case scenario, I would just copy them from her. I ripped off a piece of a blank page and wrote a message to Erica. Just three letters "FML." She always sat next to me so I just put it on her desk. Erica unfolded the paper, smiled and wrote back: "Come on, it's not that hard."

Maybe it wasn't that hard, maybe I was just predisposed. I hated math and trigonometry. Seeing this crap made me angry. Seriously, hasn't anyone noticed that mathematical knowledge stops being useful for daily life after 7th grade? Maybe my rage was the blinding factor that wouldn't let me understand any of the contents on the board. But that feeling wasn't going to change. If math was a physical entity I would beat the living crap out of it.

Erica giggled at my look of concentration and sent me another note. "Fine, you can come to my place this afternoon ;)"

During lunch, Erica and I were talking about how bizarre it was that our history teacher looked exactly like the fat guy that stole Woody from Toy Story 2 when I noticed Samantha was walking toward our table, but with some hesitance. I've seen that look a lot before—she was coming over to ask me out or give me some pretext for me to go to her house. I interrupted Erica. "*Mi cielo*, there's a teenage girl coming this way, probably with the intentions of talking to me. I would appreciate it if you behave accordingly." I had to make that request so Erica wouldn't blow Samantha off. Erica was a bit of a jealous psycho-harpy: whenever she was with me and another girl came by she practically snarled. She either hugged me or held my hand or my leg and answered whatever questions were directed to me. Nine out of ten girls that I met in that situation walked away.

Samantha was a year younger than me, blond and about the same size as Erica. We had talked at a few parties before, but when I met her I was sort of committed. At this point though, I was a free man and without plans for the weekend.

Samantha reached our table and stood there, waiting for me to notice her. The messed up thing about girls that like you is that the less attention you pay to them, the more attention they pay to you. Confident girls, like Samantha here, are used to getting what they want delivered to them. Yeah, well so am I. I had to ignore her to take from her the choice of ignoring me. If that switch of roles is performed successfully all you have to do is wait.

She closed her eyes and sighed. "Adam Lacroft."

The white flag. Now, I acknowledge her. "Anne Murray," I said, standing up to hug her.

"I hope you're kidding."

I suppose she was wondering if I actually remembered her name. "What?" I exaggerated a tone of surprise. "Your name isn't Anne?"

Samantha stared at me, but she was smiling.

They loved this game. Sometimes I really didn't remember their names and they ended up telling me, but I could almost feel Erica's eyes burning through me so I gave up the joke. "Of course I remember, Sammy. We made out at Sean's party, right?"

She blushed. "Not really, we just talked." That last part was addressed to Erica and then Samantha turned back to me. "I was wondering if," she said, "look, I'm really having trouble with math this semester and on Monday I have a test. And since you already saw all this last year, I was hoping you could come to my place on Sunday and help me out."

Erica disguised her laughter by coughing loudly.

Samantha naively asked if she was ok. Erica nodded then drank some water. "That sounds like a great idea!" Erica said. "I'm sure Adam can help you." Erica gave me an evil smile. "What was your overall grade in Math last year? D? D+?"

"B+" I said, emphasizing the "B" sound.

"Anne," I said to Samantha with a wink, "I'll make sure you get an A." Then I sat down, hoping she would leave and Erica couldn't damage the situation anymore.

Thankfully, Samantha got the message. "You have my phone number, right?"

I took out my phone. "Right here," I said, showing her the contact list: "Samantha Vane." Then I wrote next to her name, "The girl that attacked me at Sean's party."

She rolled her eyes. "We've never kissed, Adam. Call me on Sunday then. See you later."

I watched her as she walked away and then turned to Erica. "Why?"

"Why wha—" The bell rang and Erica made good use of it. "Oh, look at the time. Chemistry quiz. I have to go. I'll meet you at 3:30 by your car," she said as she put on her backpack. "You can give me a ride home, right?"

"I'm not sure you've earned it."

"Well you're coming anyways." Erica was yelling back to me as she ran out of the cafeteria. "You have to study for that test tomorrow!"

At 3:30 I walked out to the parking lot and Erica was waiting for me, sitting on the hood of my car. It was a used, scarlet Dodge, nothing luxurious, but it got me from A to B.

"You wouldn't be sitting there if you knew what I've done on it," I said as I opened the door for her.

"Adam, please, you haven't done anything on the

hood or anywhere in the car for that matter. I'm not like these idiots that fall blindly for all of your bullshit." I chuckled as I got in, then I turned on the car. She was right. I hadn't done anything. This was the sort of thing that made me proud of the relationship I had with her.

"You know I can always tell when you're lying," she added, poking my nose playfully.

She had told me a few years ago that I always did this thing with my nose when I lied or when I felt embarrassed. That I scrunched it involuntarily. I've never noticed, none of my friends have and I even asked my mom once and she told me she didn't know what I was talking about. Erica was the only one that could see it.

It took just a few minutes to get to Erica's house. "Mom, I'm here!" she shouted as we walked in. "Adam gave me a ride, he came over to study."

Her mother was cleaning some dishes, but she dried her hands and came to greet us. "Hi, sweetie," she said to her daughter and gave her a kiss on the cheek. Then she assaulted me with a hug. *"Adam, mi amor!"*

"Señora Novessel, chevere verla," I said as soon as she released me for air.

"Darling, you've known me long enough, no Mrs. Novessel. Olga, okay?" She laughed. "How's everything? It's been a while since you came over. *¿Cómo se porta Erica contigo? ¿Bien?"*

The Novessel family came from Argentina and Erica understood Spanish perfectly, but she had a weird American accent. Olga and I made fun of it, to the point that Erica avoided speaking Spanish in our presence.

"Oh you know, school and stuff. Erica, well she's kind of mean most of the time, it's getting harder to put up with her everyday."

"Erica!"

"It's not true, Mom." Erica was always annoyed by

how easily Olga believed everything I said. "We have a big test tomorrow, Mom. If you'll excuse us…." Erica walked toward the stairs. "Adam? Are you coming or is Olga going to explain high school trigonometry to you?"

I winked at Olga then followed Erica. I loved this house. Olga was a real estate agent and I'm not sure what her husband did, but evidently it was working well for them. Near the entrance there was a large living room with windows that occupied most of the wall. The kitchen looked like it had been pulled straight out of a fancy catalogue: marble counters, wooden cabinets, silver faucets and a fridge the size of my bathroom. The entire theme of the house was "modern living," so it was filled with matching pieces of stylish furniture in black and white. They had a music room in the back of the house with a beautiful, black piano. I had peacefully fallen asleep there many times while listening to Erica play. On the upper floor we passed Mr. Novessel's study, a TV room and Mr. and Mrs. Novessel's bedroom before we got to Erica's room. I opened her chamber door and bowed to indicate that ladies go first. My mom raised a proper gentleman. Then I dropped my backpack next to her desk and jumped on her large bed.

"Adam, get up! You came over to study."

I snored loudly in response and hugged one of her pillows. "Oh, Samantha," I moaned. "You dirty girl."

Erica giggled and sat next to me. "Come on, Adam, be serious. I have to go to dinner with my family in about three hours. That's all I'm asking you for, three hours."

Erica, let it go. I'll just sleep here while you make some notes and take your notebook home when you're done."

"Okay, you win. No studying," she said as leaned

over me.

Yay…. Wait—what?

She put one of her hands behind my neck and started caressing me.

"Erica, wha—"

"Shh! Lately I've noticed this is the only sort of thing that I can do to get your full attention." She stretched her thin body on top of mine. Now I was confused and turned on. Terrible combination.

"Let's see: you can either get your lazy ass off the bed and next to the desk or you can walk downstairs, say goodbye to your good friend Olga and fail your test tomorrow, miserably."

Looking at my mouth, Erica moved closer, but her lips grazed over my cheek then up to my ear. "And I do feel so very happy when I rescue my friends from mediocre grades. Who knows? You just might get a reward." She planted a small kiss on my neck and got off of the bed.

This was cruel. On top of my emotional feelings for her she was now abusing my animal instincts. I sat up slowly to give myself some time. Arguing or begging would be futile; the only way I was going to get some more action was by cooperating with our study session and passing the test tomorrow. I was somewhat angry but all I could do was shake it off. I pulled up a chair next to her and put my trigonometry notebook on the table. I looked at her with a smirk and caught her looking at my lips. It wasn't the first time she had done something like that to me, the others just weren't as intense but it had happened before. The sexual tension between us was growing and she was starting to give in. After this, I had a feeling I wouldn't be studying with Samantha on Sunday.

I decided to stop thinking about everything else and focus completely on passing the test. I needed to ace this bastard. Erica explained the exercises over and over again to me. She told me that the key to it was memorizing the equations and functions and then knowing where to use each. She wrote down all of the necessary formulas, tips and examples on a sheet of paper for me and drew a big title at the top of the page. "ClearValley Senior Year Trigonometry for Dummies (Adam)." Before I noticed it my three hours were up and Erica had to get ready for dinner with her parents. She walked me out to the car.

"Thanks, Erica, I'm actually feeling safe for tomorrow," I said.

In her terrible Spanish, she answered, *"de nada."*

I opened the car door.

"Adam?"

I turned around and we looked at each other in silence. She walked up to me and gave me a kiss on the cheek. "Text me when you get home, okay?"

I nodded then I got in the car and watched her as she walked back into the house. I lingered there for a minute. So did her kiss.

All the way home I thought about that kiss. It was completely different from what had happened in her room in the afternoon. It was so cute, so childish, and something from that little girl inside her brought out the little boy in me.

I got home and finished the homework she had given me on the "ClearValley Senior Year Trigonometry for Dummies" worksheet. Then I took a shower and went straight to bed.

I woke up early that next morning, happy with an idea; I was going to make something special for Erica this weekend. Starting today, maybe even come clean about my feelings for her. I suddenly felt sure that if I grew up a little more inside, just enough to make thoughtful adult decisions, I could start something with her, something much more important than anything I'd had before. I would have acted sooner though, had I known that on Saturday night I was going to die.

The Girl I Like

Every time I relive what happened to me I like to stay a little bit longer in the happy parts, the parts that you overlook until they're no longer available.

On that Friday morning, test day, I was enjoying a few minutes of pre-school relaxation in my bed when I received a text from Erica. "Don't forget my English notebook, genius."

I swear, I think she's sneaking these things in my backpack without me noticing. "Are we going to make a habit out of this?" I texted back.

I had a simple bedroom: one bed where I barely fit, a night table on each side, a desk where I did my homework and a medium-sized TV set attached to the wall. My bed was small for a reason, it made it impossible for two people to sit or lie in it comfortably separated, which generally helped speed things up.

I scavenged through my closet, looking for a shirt in a wearable state. After dismissing a few, I approved one and started changing for school.

Erica texted me again: "That wouldn't be so bad. I could be like your personal alarm clock."

"Well, you're just as annoying."

I went to the bathroom for my clean-up routine. First, I empty the night's fuel reservoirs; I like to try and see from how far away I can get it in the toilet. My personal record is three feet and seven inches, but that day I had a feeling I could break it. Or not.

Damn it, I made a mess.

After that, I brush my teeth and wash my hands and face. I learned one day that if you use liquid soap, like the standard kind in public bathrooms, you can make huge bubbles. All you have to do is rub some soap on your hands, let some water trickle onto it and then run the tip of your thumb from the beginning of your index finger until both the tips are touching, like when divers do the "OK" sign underwater. There should be a layer of soap covering that gap and all you have to do is blow softly. After a few attempts I managed to make one as big as my face. I admired it for a few seconds before it popped.

Then I let the water fill up the sink and plunge my head in the small pool, pretending someone is trying to drown me in it. That last part ensured I was fully awake for school. I know this is all very childish, but then again, I never really planned on growing up. My clean-up routine ended with me striking some poses to the mirror and signing off with a wink and an "Adam, you handsome devil."

I walked out of the bathroom then went downstairs and found my dad making breakfast. I got told all the time that I looked just like my father when he was my age. That means he was probably a handsome devil too. He's almost an exact, but older, version of me; we have the same cinnamon skin, square jaw and big smile. The only difference is the eye color. His are olive green and mine are black. Oh, and the small beauty spot just behind the right eye. Those two things I got from my mom. Oh, another thing was our hair. While mine was messy and abundant, my dad's started to bail when he was younger so now he keeps it cut short.

I hugged my dad and gave him a kiss on the bald spot above his forehead.

"Dad, did you ever have hair?"

"Fun fact: loss of hair is a hereditary condition," he said, pulling mine. "And I lost most of it when I was eighteen, so enjoy your last year with yours. Go set the table, I made you food."

I grabbed two plates and he served us both scrambled eggs and toast.

"You have a trigonometry test today, if your mom isn't mistaken."

I had just taken a mouthful of food, so I nodded.

"Are you up for it?"

"I think so, Erica helped me study. Oh, and speaking of Erica, I need the terrace tonight, Dad."

"Oooh, the terrace?"

"Dad, show some respect for the terrace."

Whenever I really liked a girl I brought her to our terrace for a picnic or a dinner. There was really nothing particularly fancy about it, it's just that girls like that crap. A clear sky with stars or a fiery sunset—they make possible a psychological chain reaction that leads to an emotional turn-on.

"Well, good luck with that," my dad said and then finished his last piece of toast. "By the way, I'm going to be in the house tonight, I'm bringing my work home. Try to keep things PG-13."

I felt sorry for my mom sometimes because even though my dad was in his forties it was like having another teenager around the house. He was always pulling pranks, making silly jokes with me and annoying his wife. My mom told me once that when I was baby, she arrived early from work and my dad was hanging me out over the railing of the terrace, singing "The Circle of Life."

"Adam, are you finished?"

I could always tell from the look on my dad's face when he was about to make a parentally questionable proposition.

"Drag race to school?"

See what I mean? He wasn't kidding: we actually did race a few times and, like everything illegal and dangerous, it was extremely fun.

"Arthur!" my mom shouted from the hall. "He's going to take it seriously one of these days." She

18

walked into the kitchen. "How am I supposed to tell him to be responsible when his father is encou–"

My dad shut her up with a kiss. She was resistant for a second, but then she relaxed.

"Good morning, love," he said softly.

"Good morning, Artie."

I could tell it was taking her some effort to stay angry at him.

"We'll talk about this later, Arthur. Adam, go brush your teeth. I'll wash up here."

Behind her back, my dad mouthed, "Hurry up, I'll wait for you at the end of the street" and left.

Ten minutes later I was on the way to school, but there was no drag racing. When I passed the end of the street my dad wasn't there. He probably couldn't wait for me any longer and continued on to his work.

After parking my car in the teachers' parking lot, I walked straight to the chemistry lab. It was one of the few classes Erica wasn't in with me and I arrived just as the bell rang. I didn't pay too much attention to the experiment we were doing and I let my partner do most of the work because I was somewhat nervous about the trigonometry test. Well, to be honest, I was thinking more about Erica than the exam. I lost myself between memories and daydreams, plotting every aspect of the dinner tonight. She had a thing for constellations and according to The Weather Channel it was going to be a cloudless night. So I was recalling the few facts I knew about astrology that I could entertain her with.

1.The Milky Way is called the Milky Way because, according to Greek mythology, Hera was breastfeeding Zeus's bastard son Hercules by mistake and when she realized this, she pulled him away quickly and a shot of boob-milk just stuck itself in the sky. (Yeah I know, messed up. I'm pretty sure Greece was the first society to secretly have discovered weed.)

2.Ophiuchus, the 13th sign of the Zodiac. I personally think it's the most retarded thing in the 21st century after music-playing toothbrushes. How the hell did they miss that? How did someone just go like, "Well, what do you know? There's a constellation right there"? It's literally an ugly heptagon with a random line sticking out of one of the angles and the figure assigned to it is an old man with a huge boa constrictor between his legs. (Shocker, not the Greeks, it was the Romans this time.)

3.This won't do… I need more fun-facts.

Before I could think up anymore, chemistry was over so I headed toward classroom 47 or, as Mr. Connor likes to call it, "Where the joyous odyssey of knowledge awaits." Faced with the choice, I would seriously consider going through the real Odyssey over spending an hour listening to Mr. Connor profess his love for math.

"You know, if I was a stranger I would think you're having deep thoughts about the Greater Good." Erica appeared on my right.

"How do you know that I'm not?"

"I'm pretty sure there's some mild swearing going on in there," she said, watching me from the corner of her eye.

My reaction was received as an indication that she was getting warmer.

"All right! Now, considering our actual schedule I'm guessing the swearing is directed at Mr. Connor or one of his cheesy slogans."

I kept walking calmly. I wanted to see how far she could get.

"Hmmm… 'Math is such a beauty'?"

I showed no response.

"Nah, that wouldn't piss you off, it's one of the

more elaborate, like a random reference to something that has absolutely nothing to do with math. Wait!" She employed this dorky dance she reserved for the recognition of good food and victory. "'Where the joyous odyssey of knowledge awaits!'"

"I'm impressed."

"You look so cute when you're concentrating." She giggled. "I'm not sitting anywhere near you during the test: I can't do an exam seriously if you're there looking like you're solving the Grandfather Paradox."

Which was fine, because I wanted to avoid the temptation of cheating. We went in, took our seats and Mr. Connor dictated his usual speech before an important test.

"Students, you know the drill, there's nothing new to add: everything we saw in class is right there. It is an individual exam, not the UN's General Assembly. Meaning no talking, no whispering, no notes. Break these rules and I get to fail you." He stopped to gaze at the class, I think because he liked to see a pre/post exam face. "Success for those who studied and luck for those who didn't. You may begin."

I flipped the exam over hesitantly, afraid that I would find all of the problems structured with the few procedures that were the most difficult for me. To my relief, Mr. Connor wasn't lying. Everything on it we had seen in class and done in homework assignments. Not exactly of course, but similar elements and situations that, thanks to the ClearValley Senior Year Trigonometry worksheet, I could now face head-on. An hour and twenty minutes later I finished, left my exam on Mr. Connor's desk and walked out of the classroom. I waited outside a few minutes until Erica joined me. "I have no clue of what I just did in there," she said.

"If you get anything higher than a C, I'm beating you up behind the cafeteria," I said to her, trying to cheer her up. Then we discussed all of the results. Most of them we got the same answer so I finally convinced her to relax.

"You know, I think our overall performance deserves a celebration. You as a teacher and me as, well, me." This was the excuse for the evening I had planned.

She lifted one of her eyebrows. "I guess so... it's not like I have a choice, do I? I'm sure this isn't something spontaneous. But you know I babysit till five, after that I'm all yours."

"Great, come by the house at seven. Dress nice or don't dress at all. I'm fine with the latter."

She laughed and we went off to different classes.

At three o'clock, I rushed for my car. I didn't want to bump into her. I guess I wanted to build up her expectations. As soon as I got home I started working on the terrace. I assembled the plastic table we have in our garage, washed it and set it up with a nice tablecloth, some candles and the expensive silverware my mom had in case a count ever decided to drop by our house. At six o'clock, I took a shower and then started working on the dinner so it would be ready by the time Erica arrived. As soon as I was done I dressed up: pants, shirt, tie, I even combed my hair. About ten minutes later the doorbell rang. I was still engaged with the finishing touches, so I let my dad greet her and let her in.

I heard her steps on the stairs and turned around. She was gorgeous; the dark eyeliner exalted her eyes and her wavy hair, complemented by her red dress, was loose over her shoulders. The few freckles in her cheeks accentuated the cuter side of her, though it was hard to imagine there was a cute side. I'm sure she wasn't aiming at sensuality, but anything she wore ended up being seductive.

"Wow. You look amazing," I stuttered.

My heart started pounding harder in my chest. It had been a while since I felt nervous around a girl.

Erica blushed and walked toward me slowly, looking at the table and the terrace. "Adam, this is so cute."

I pulled out her chair and she sat down. Erica looked at the two covered plates, the bread basket and the glass wine bottle. "I didn't know you cooked."

"Of course I cook, Erica. You remember last summer's tragedy."

"You mean when your Xbox broke down?" She burst out in laughter. "You called me, crying, that day.

"Well of course I cried. My Xbox was useless, I had to euthanize it."

"What does that have to do with you cooking?" she asked when she caught her breath.

"In my depression I couldn't sleep well anymore and I found consolation in late-night reruns of the Food Network…. If you make one more joke about my Xbox, I'm escorting you out of the house."

Those were the worst two weeks of my vacation; my Xbox met a horrible and sudden end, Erica was out of the country and I was having a bad streak with dates.

"Okay, let's see it," she said as she uncovered her plate, revealing a lovely serving of pasta. Macaroni and cheese, to be more specific. "Seriously? Mac and cheese? Wow, the Food Network is going through some bad times."

I took her glass and served from the bottle, but there wasn't wine in it. I made fun of the way the waiters do it when they serve it, twisting the bottle at the end.

Erica examined it and then took a sip. "Capri Sun? Adam, what are you, like seven?"

"At times," I answered as I sat down. "It was your

favorite when we were kids, right? Cherry."

I didn't make macaroni and cheese because that's the only thing I learned from the Food Network. I think everything through.

In 1998, the Japanese horror movie Ringu was released. Based on the novel by Koji Suzuki, the film told the story about a videotape that anyone who watched it mysteriously died seven days later. Some asshole named Ehren Kruger decided to do a script and worked with Director Gore Verbinski to release a remake in 2002 that the world would come to know as The Ring. That shit should be illegal. Somewhere in 2003 Erica and I decided to watch it because we thought I would be fun. It was not fun. We weren't able to sleep or bathe or be unaccompanied for a goddamn month. But what we went through that month was nothing in comparison to that night. We were so scared we turned on every single light in the house. TVs were out of the question. We came to the grim conclusion that if we passed out we would die, so we did anything we could think of to stay awake. It was eleven p.m. when we finished the movie—the sun rises at six. We had to endure seven long hours of raw fear. We danced, we drew, we sang, we showered. We walked around the house with these cardboard shields so we could cover ourselves when we passed a mirror. That wasn't the ghost's MO, but you can't be too careful. By four a.m. our determination wasn't weakened, but our energy was. Pleading to my parents for protection and nurture was no longer an option: they got the sick satisfaction of saying "We told you guys that was a strong movie." So, in our starvation, we stormed the kitchen; cookies, cereal, nothing was spared but we wanted more.

It was then that I had seen the macaroni and cheese box.

We were no longer children, dependent on their parents' will to prepare a meal. We had discovered fire. It became the official dish of our movie marathons, from which horror movies were banned. Of course it's been ages since we had done that, since she became the reason for inappropriate thoughts in boy's head's and I became a fulfiller of these thoughts in other girl's realities. I imagined the memories that the dinner was supposed to arouse popping into her head as I lost myself in the complexity of her eyes. We stayed like that a few seconds.

"Buen Provecho," I said as I picked up my fork.

We talked about trivial things at first: friends, that terrible summer, music, our plan to inform the school board that the history teacher might steal the preschooler's hopes and dreams, like he did in Toy Story 2. Eventually we finished eating, so I cleared the table and we lay down on the floor to gaze at the sky.

"Wow, the stars are gorgeous tonight," Erica said.

"They're just jealous. They're mad cause you out shone them," I said, sort of regretting it after the words came out.

She snorted a laugh. "Well, that was lame."

I laughed too. It was kind of cheesy.

"I was starting to think you had every line, every scenario planned, Adam. I've always wondered how your dates played out."

"I always leave room for improvisation, Erica. And if this was a date we would probably be in my room making out by now.'

"Oh, Heavens, no! How would the stars feel about that? Are they jealous of me or of you?"

"De mi, obviamente. They're ganged up waiting for you to leave the house: Orion's crew is there on the right, the Northern Boss with his goons." I pointed randomly across the sky. "And Ursa Major looks like

she's in the mood for some ass-kicking." I knew those constellations existed; I had no idea where they were though.

"I'd be willing to face their wrath, over the right reasons." She turned to face me. "Would you?"

I was going to answer the question but her eyes got my heart racing and the joke lost its innocence. The way she said that last question—this was it, this was the time to go for it. So why didn't I? I usually rocked at reading this sort of crap, why was I doubting the opportunity? God damn it, Adam, get it together, make a move.

Erica's phone went off.

Too late, I missed it. If I wanted to do anything that was the moment and I blew it. Shit happens when you don't stick to the plan, Adam. I felt the anxiety swelling up in my chest; disappointment, rage at myself, fear that I might not get another shot.

"That was my mom," Erica frowned. "She's on her way."

Normally I would have seen right away that she was disappointed because nothing happened, but I was in lockdown, I couldn't rely on my judgment.

"I want to help you clean up before I go," Erica said as she sat up.

We brought all the plates down to the kitchen, no talking. I was thinking of a way to salvage the situation, but nothing came to my head. We sat on the stairs in silence, waiting for her mom to honk the horn when she arrived.

Erica pointed at a wooden box in the corner. "What's that?"

"That's my Xbox." I knew the words engraved on the lid by heart. "'Here lies a friend and the gateway to many others. 2009-2010.'"

She rolled her eyes. "You're such a child."

We heard a car stopping in front of the house, so we walked toward the door. I was putting my hand on the doorknob when Erica put her arms around my neck and kissed me. I reached for her hips and held her tight.

How the hell was this happening? I wasn't going to stop it for anything, but I still wondered. My confidence came back in a rush, along with happiness I couldn't contain.

I kissed her softly, unable to arrange my thoughts. She pulled back and looked at me with a huge smile then she punched me in the chest. "Why didn't you kiss me upstairs, you idiot."

I opened my mouth and stuttered.

She gave me her evil smile. "You panicked. Adam Lacroft panicked. Wow, I'm either a very lucky girl or a very ugly one."

I tried to say something again, but she stopped me with another kiss.

"You're clearly not in the state to say anything at all, so I'm not going to let you ruin it. Take a shower, go sleep and call me in the morning." She finished with a wink and then opened the door.

Where Corpses Lie

"Adam, where are you taking me? We've been on the road for like an hour."

The trip was supposed to be shorter, around thirty minutes, but I had taken a few wrong turns. She probably suspected that, but she couldn't really know because she was blindfolded, so when she asked me I denied it.

"Can I please take this off now?"

"No, you can't," I said without looking at her. I didn't want to miss the right exit again. "I told you, it's a surprise."

"Adam this is sweet, but Vegas is like seventeen hours away. I want to at least enjoy the view."

"Well, someone is a little overconfident. You haven't even proposed." I swung wide because I almost missed the next turn. "Jesus Christ, I can't concentrate! Next time I'm putting you out with ether after I blindfold you."

"You couldn't tell ether from water, Adam. You would probably put yourself out first."

I stopped the car. "That's it, I'm taking you back."

"Noo, I'm sorry." She gave me a kiss on the cheek to go with her apology and promised she would behave until we arrived at wherever we were headed.

My destination wasn't Vegas, of course. It was a graveyard on the edge of the city, one that I had gone to since I was a kid. It was possible Erica had visited it at some point in her life, but I had never heard her talk about it so she probably didn't know of it. It was one of my favorite places in this city and it's safe to say it was almost mine because I rarely saw another person other than myself visit it. It was inhabited mostly by people who died when I would have rather lived, the second half of the nineteenth century. And because they died in a time where class and beauty were held in a much different place than where they are today, it appeared that each family had chosen a grave that would outdo in every way all the others around it. The graveyard was about a hundred acres of marble, granite, iron and bronze structures that pledged to protect the remains of something useless to most, but worth the world to a few, at the cost of their own degradation. I found them inspiring and Erica was someone I wanted to share that with.

I pulled in through the big iron gates and parked in the desolate lot. I grabbed my backpack and the picnic basket and escorted her all the way to the spot I wanted to set up in. It was a twenty-minute walk, but every time Erica complained I hit her in the back of the head with a stick. I learned that from the cattle wranglers in Venezuela.

We reached a section in the northeastern corner, where there's a lake. Half of it was surrounded by hills populated with those funeral edifications and the other half was a clearing. Basked in the sunset was a columbarium as imposing as the Pantheon in Rome. In the half with the clearing, there was a large sycamore tree in whose shade we were going to set up camp. Close to it there was a wooden rowboat for two.

"We're here, you may take off the blindfold."

"Finally!" She undid the knot.

"Adam, where are we?"

"I know it's kind of weird, but I come here all the time," I said as I stretched a blanket over the grass.

It was autumn then and the cemetery was orange, courtesy of the sunset that lit up the graves and the leaves of the half-dead trees. "I feel happy here, I think it's the most beautiful place I know. I know it may not seem that way at first, but I see more to it. I wanted to show it to you, so you can see it, too."

"I see it," she whispered.

I opened the basket, but we paid little attention to the food. We were too busy exploring this new side of us. It was like we were meeting for the first time, though in our introduction and during our conversation we used few words. Wrapped around each other we kissed, held hands, played with each other's toes. I bit her ear, drew constellations between her twenty-three freckles. She named my beauty spot Shaggy, kissed the tip of my nose, pinched my butt. We laughed. Love has no age, but this sort of thing can only be for the young. Some people might say, "This is getting kind of gay." Well no, it's the fucking definition of heterosexual and such people are losing out in life. This feeling, the secretion of endorphins and other hormones that cloud our better judgment... there's nothing else in the world like it. After what felt like hours, I managed to get her off of me so we could move on to the next part of the date.

"Where are you going?" she said, clutching my leg.

"I'm going to get the boat, so we can ride in it."

"Do we have to? We were fine right here."

"Yeah, but the boat is part of the date. The date won't be complete without it."

I stood up and walked to the boat. I dragged it a little closer to us, got in, and crossed my arms waiting for Erica to join me.

"Adam, I really don't want to."

"Get on the boat, woman."

"God! Fine," she said and I realized her tone was not playful at all.

She stood up and took a few steps, but before she got to the water she stopped. Something flickered across her face. I didn't understand then why she would feel afraid of going near the water.

"Erica, do you not know how to swim?"

"Of course I know, it's not that."

"What's wrong then?"

The concern on her face was obvious. She knew that I knew she was afraid, so she didn't bother lying anymore. "*I* can't. Just don't ask anymore, Adam, I can't explain it."

"I'm not going to ask, Erica." I pulled the blindfold out of my pocket and extended my hand toward her: "*¿Confías en mí, no mi cielo?*"

She gave me a vague nod, took the blindfold from my hands and tied it around her face. I helped her get on the boat and rowed softly away from the clearing.

"Are we moving?" Erica asked, grasping firmly the rails of the boat.

"The Gloria Scott is a smooth vessel, she is," I said in a sort of pirate accent.

Good God, Adam. That was even worse than the line from yesterday.

Silence.

Erica snorted into laughter again. "You're such a geek, Adam. Enough with the weird comments, you're going to make me change my mind about us."

"Please, as if us happening was up to you."

"Wanna go through with that statement? I can find a way home."

"Be my guest," I dared her back and crossed my arms.

She took her blindfold off, stood up and noticed that we were now a few meters away from land. She looked at me, looked back at our picnic. From the look on her face, something like "I hate you" was probably passing through her head.

"*Yo tambien te quiero, linda,*" I sent back and winked. I loved these mute conversations.

She sat down again.

"Thought so," I boasted.

"Jerk."

"Stupid-head."

"Dumbass."

"Skank."

"Templar."

"Shit, you win." I laughed.

We lay down in the boat.

"Are you still scared?"

"A little."

I hugged her closer and gave her a kiss on her forehead. "Don't be."

After a few minutes she fell asleep on my chest.

I was definitely not going to study with Samantha on Sunday. A weird train of thoughts followed that conclusion. I started thinking about school and college and the future and about how none of that mattered at that moment. Not knowing what I was going to do with my life, all the choices that eventually narrowed down to basic survival, I started seeing those things as if they were going to work out by themselves. Ataraxia: peace of mind, freedom. This annoying red-headed girl gave me all of this just by falling asleep on my chest. She will always give me this. She always has.

"Rise and shine, sunshine." I scratched her head. "It's getting late, we need to leave."

She rolled off of me with a growl, put on the blindfold again, and sat down properly so I could row us back to our campsite. We picked everything up and twenty minutes later we were in the car heading home. On the way, she sorted through my CD collection, complaining that my music was not road trip music.

"Phoenix... The Strokes... The XX... The Wombats? Adam, you listen to such random music. That does not make you cooler, you know? These people are mildly famous for a reason," she said as she searched for a song that she liked or, given her tone, tolerated.

"They're mildly famous because the world sucks and talented material is discarded over popular material. Indie rock forever."

"Oh boy, here we go with the hipster crap."

"I'm sorry I like my music with actual instruments and meaningful lyrics," I said as I turned up the volume. "And Indie Rock in particular is unbelievable. It fits with so many situations, the music, the rhythm—"

"'Nobody likes real music anymore.' Cry me a river, Adam."

"Okay, you need to live this. Let's do it."

"Do what?"

"We're going into an Indie trance."

"Dear Lord." She buried her face in her hands. "What the hell is an Indie trance?"

"Words cannot describe it," I replied dramatically and raised the volume to the fullest.

Erica closed her eyes and we listened attentively. The guitar, bass, drums: the music drowned out all thoughts. The harmony made me so happy. Erica couldn't hide her smile either. That moment was perfect—nothing could ruin it.

I was pulled out of the trance by a bright light, two actually, coming from my left. It was too late when I realized what they were. The second the glass broke and the metal bent everything went silent.

The last voluntary thing I was able to do was hold Erica's hand.

The Higher Authority

I woke up relieved, rested, just like after a good night's sleep when you don't get the urge to stay in bed longer. It took me a bit to recall what had happened before I blacked out, but then I saw it all again: the crash, fire, broken glass and Erica lying next to me on the ground.

"Erica!" I screamed out, jumping off of the bed. I was about to shout her name for a second time when I noticed I wasn't alone. There was a girl sitting next to my bed.

"Well good morning, sleepyhead," she said cheerfully.

I stared at her. What kind of stupid nurse is she? She clearly didn't know how to deal with patients that had just suffered a near-death experience.

"What hospital is this? Where's Erica—the girl that was with me in the crash?"

"If you look around, Mr. Lacroft, you'll realize you're not in a hospital."

Her last comment brought to my attention the room I was in. There were no other beds or machines near me, no curtains, no IVs in my arm; in fact, I was still in the same clothes from the crash. I was in a small, white room, with only my bed and the chair the girl was seated in. If this isn't a hospital, what is it? Then I took a longer look at her. She was gorgeous. She was wearing a short, black dress with big white polka dots on the edge of the skirt. She had cute, round cheeks and dark eyes that matched the black hair that ran down her back. Because of this she looked about sixteen, seventeen maybe, but I knew she had to be older, probably starting her twenties.

"Where is Erica?"

"She's not here, silly. You came alone."

That relaxed me somewhat. Wherever I was, at least Erica was safe. "Where am I then?"

"Gosh, I never really know how to say this. The thing is," she interrupted herself with a giggle, "you're dead."

I did not punch her in the face solely because she was a girl, a really hot one, but the joking around was calling for it. "Oh, that explains it."

Maybe this is some weird hospital testing a way to deal with traumatized patients. They joke around a bit, let you take the edge off of the whole situation and try to make you forget about all the problems that come after an accident. Well, at least until you heal up.

"You're not dead yet, you'll still be alive for the next twenty minutes, but I brought you here now because I have a proposition." She laced her fingers together and put her hands on her lap.

I didn't like the patronizing gesture. This was getting really weird; she was dragging the joke out too much.

She must have noticed I thought so because she got more serious. "It's all right, few people believe it when I tell them."

After she said this, an excruciating amount of pain came over my body. My head starting pounding so hard I thought it was going to burst. I tried to raise my hands to my temples but my left arm wasn't responding, something was lodged in it. I was on the highway again. I felt the rough surface under my hands. A few feet away from us was my car, flipped over and smashed from one side. There were two paramedics kneeling next to me, pointing flashlights at my face and examining my body. I couldn't really hear anything, just a dull ringing. I managed to turn my face away from them and I got a glimpse of Erica being held back by two police officers. She was trying to tell me something, but I couldn't understand what she was saying. Just as quickly as I was brought there, I was back in the white room in front of the girl.

"Seventeen minutes," she said as she looked down at her watch.

I turned around looking for an exit, but found only the blank wall that surrounded the room. I was able to process one emotion only: fear.

"Who are you?" I asked, trying to sound menacing. "And what the hell is this place?"

"Come on, Mr. Lacroft, you're a smart kid. I'm sure you can pull the pieces together. Your last memory is crashing in a car, you just witnessed yourself and you're injured, bleeding on the highway…." She raised her eyebrow waiting for me to answer my own question and then frowned at my silence.

"I'm what awaits at the end." She added in a deep voice, mocking a storyteller, "The one thing no man can avoid." She giggled at my unchanging look of incomprehension. "I'm Death, silly."

Death. Wait, Death? What the hell was she saying? Death isn't a person, it isn't a being, it's just an action, right? I was probably in some messed up dream, asleep in a hospital, waiting out the effects of the cocktail of drugs they had to put in me to keep me alive.

My train of thought was interrupted by her childish voice. "Looks like you still need some more proof."

The pain started coming back to my limbs, but slower, as if to convince me of the reality of the sensation.

"No, no, no!" But it was too late, my body was paralyzed. I screamed but nothing came out, I don't think my mouth even opened. It was like my body was responding inside my head, but in reality I couldn't move it. I was being carried into an ambulance. This time I got a view of the crash. We had been hit by a black car that was now wrecked and in flames. Its hood and most of the front of the vehicle was gone so it must have exploded after the impact. The driver wasn't in the car, maybe he died in the explosion. I hoped he did. Thanks to that asshole I was experiencing weird trances and illusions of depictions of death.

This wasn't a dream though, or a random trance. You would think that if some girl you've never seen before came up to you and claimed to be Death you'd have a hard time believing her, but I didn't. After feeling and seeing what I had felt and seen, trust me, you too would be persuaded otherwise. In that moment the tide of emotions in me changed, fear morphed into curiosity and I felt like asking her everything: Where did I go after this? Did she greet everyone who died? Why was she so damn hot? But I didn't think that was the goal of our meeting and her look confirmed that I should be using my little time left listening to her. I wondered if she could read my mind, because it sure felt like it. What else could she do? I mean she was Death, she must have some array of supernatural privileges.

She had said "seventeen minutes." She must have had a reason for keeping me alive and revealing her existence to me. Even though my mind was racing with all sorts of thoughts about this girl, I knew I had to clear my head. "Let's hear it."

"Just so you know, I can't read your mind."

I tried to hide the surprise on my face, but I guess I failed.

"Everyone reacts differently, but I can tell what kind of reaction you're having. People like you, smart people, are filled with curiosity. They accept the situation is out of their control and venture to gain the most out of it; they cope with the whole thing quite nicely." She looked down. "Some run desperately, some cry, some pray. The latter offend me; once you're in here it's all up to me, there IS NO higher authority." She raised her voice angrily in that last statement, but calmed down again. "Besides, this God guy didn't stop them from coming to me—never has—so why would he step in because they cry out poems? But enough about me, we have to get down to business, Mr. Lacroft."

The way she talked, as if she was selling me a car, disturbed me. She was an odd image for Death; cute voice, gorgeous face. She reminded me of a preschool teacher. She spoke so comfortably about it she made you feel unsure if any of it was actually happening.

"Gee, Mr. Lacroft sounds so very formal. If things go the way I think they will you and I will be seeing a lot more of each other. So what can I call you? Adam, Adam Lacroft, Adi, A.L.?"

"Adam is just dandy." I looked into her empty black eyes. "So what should I call you? Persephone? Atropos? Mrs. Reaper?" That last one made her smile. If she was human she might have even blushed.

"Eve sounds rather nice. I think we would make a lovely couple under different circumstances," she answered with a wink.

"All right then, Eve, you said you had a proposition and I think I'm running out of time," I said, trying to keep it cool. It was funny, Eve might have been Death, but that didn't stop me from wanting to flirt with her.

"Oh yes, of course. Well you see, Adam, I found your death quite unnecessary. Tragic even. You were minding your own life and it's not fair that some old drunk should end it. But I can't give it back to you just like that. Nothing in life, or in this case, death, is free. You have to do something for me in return."

"I'm afraid I don't play the fiddle."

This brought out another smile. The kind of smile

that makes both boys and men fall in love.

"No worries, I make deals only. They tend to have more... expected results. And your deal is a simple one, I only want you to prevent your death."

I was going to ask exactly how that was possible since, well, I already died, but she put one finger on my lips.

"Sh-sh-sh! Adam, sweetie, let me finish. I want you to stop your death from ever happening. I'm giving you a second chance. You are going to get three days to find the man responsible for your death and deal with him. Let me make it perfectly clear that preventing your current fate isn't as simple as hiding in a room until the deadline is up. This isn't a favor, it's an exchange, and there are terms that have to be met— otherwise I won't comply on my part." Eve pronounced this last part particularly slowly and without the cheery tone that she had used when she introduced herself.

She looked into my eyes. "So, Adam, what is it you have to do when you leave this room?"

"Get a drink?" I chuckled and waited for that beautiful smile. But it didn't come. I tried to look somewhere else and think of a better joke, but I couldn't keep my eyes off of hers. The way she stared into me was frightening.

"I have to find the man that crashed into us and kill him."

Those words came out of my mouth, but it wasn't me who said them. It couldn't have been, I mean, it sounded so cold, so inhumanly determined. Sure, I didn't give a damn if he died in the crash or if he died anywhere for that matter. But I didn't want to kill him—why should I? I had a motive, but not the motivation. A man I didn't know, who was drunk, and we had the bad luck to be on his path that night. Why did I say I was going to kill him?

Eve had said, "You are going to get three days to search and find the man responsible for your death and deal with him." I hadn't even thought of what I was going to do with him once I found him, probably try to find some way to explain the situation to him and... and then what? I couldn't stop thinking about that sentence that had come out of my mouth.

"Wait, what? Why do I have to kill him? I mean he's a prick, but can't I get him arrested or something?"

"I'm surprised, I didn't think you were the forgiving type. This man ended your life, he was close to ending your friend's as well."

"Look, I'm furious at this guy, but can't I beat the crap out of him and leave it like that? Or, you know, sue him? Let him get raped in prison, maybe murdered eventually?"

I was hoping she would change her mind. Even if I got past the fact I didn't want to kill him, there were still many other problems involved in a murder, getting away with it being a major concern. Eve curled a lock of hair behind her ear before answering. "Adam, there is a balance that has to be maintained in this thing. A life for a life, that's how it works." Then she looked down again, as if she was remembering something. "This man needs to die."

I got it then. Eve was the one who had made me say that sentence; it was as if she had welded those instructions into my brain. Those were the definite terms of our agreement. "I have to find the man that crashed into us and kill him." I had three days to do that or I would end up coming back to this room again.

"What if I say no?"

"Excuse me?" she scoffed.

I bet that was the first time someone had ever thought of declining her offer. "The paramedics are there. I'm being treated as we speak, what makes you so sure I won't survive without your help?"

She couldn't believe my question. Hell, I was doubting it too.

Eve gripped the handles of the silver metal chair so hard they started to bend to the shape of her hands.

I regretted the words the second I saw her expression. Why would she not know if I was going to make it? She's Death, jackass. Seriously, out of all the stupid cocky things you've answered to people with power over you, this was just a whole new level.

The handles were about to melt when she let go of the chair and burst in laughter.

"Adam, I haven't had this much fun in years. Come on, sweetie, you really didn't think I would have offered you this deal if you had the possibility of surviving?" She stopped a moment and stroked the chair handles, smoothing them back into their original form.

"I'm Death. I know if you're going to die or not. But your reasoning certainly amused me. There have been cases where people come this far and are brought back, especially with technology these days. But you're not one of those cases." She looked at her watch. "Three minutes. Well, you know the terms, take it or leave it."

I didn't really have a choice... or did I?

"Eve?"

"Yes, Adam?"

I think she knew what I was going to ask her. "What comes after you?"

Eve showed me that hypnotizing smile. "That would spoil the surprise, wouldn't it?"

I smiled back. Of course she wasn't going to tell me what happened in the afterlife.

"I'll take it."

"Just one more thing," she said and held out her

41

hand, waiting for me to shake it.

I was hesitant at the thought of returning to my messed up body in the ambulance. How was I supposed to recover from those injuries and hunt down and kill a grown man, perfectly capable of putting up a fight, in three days?

"Don't worry, I don't bite..."

I grinned and shook her hand.

"... hard."

I felt light warmth moving from her hand to mine, stopping at my wrist and burning somewhat stronger. I instinctively pulled my hand back. "What was that for?" I hissed.

"That's the signing of our contract."

I looked at my wrist to see if it was burned, but instead of a wound there was a symbol, sort of like a tattoo. It was a small triangle with three half-moons, one on each side and a little circle on top of each.

"That will serve as a reminder of our deal and as long as you have it on we can talk, should we need to. It's also the proof you're going to need when you wake up to remind you this actually happened."

It was clever of her to think of that. I was sure that if I had woken up without some evidence I would have thought it was all just a dream.

"You shouldn't be so skeptical, Adam. There are things in life that are beyond your understanding and, evidently, your control."

I woke up in my room; relieved, rested, just like after a good night's sleep when you don't get the urge to stay in bed longer. I sat up in my bed and it took me a bit to recall what happened before I blacked out, but then I saw it all again: the crash, the white room and Eve. I knew it had all been real, but just to check I raised my right hand to my face and there it was, the little black symbol in charge of reminding me of my encounter with Death.

The only other time in my life where death had been a tangible concern was sometime last year. I was on a plane returning home from a trip with my class when we flew right into the middle of the storm. The clouds turned coal black and the raindrops were so big it felt like pebbles were hitting the plane. The lights went out and what little we could see was thanks to the flashes from the lightning dangerously close to the plane. The strong winds caused the plane to suffer sudden drops, some for as long as ten seconds before it stabilized itself again. Erica was shrieking every time the plane lost height suddenly and I was laughing at her, raising my hands as if it was a roller coaster. That pissed her off and she had yelled at me, saying how could I joke around about the plane falling. I remember telling her: "If it did Erica, what can you do to stop it? If it does fall, chances are we're all going to die, so what use is it getting scared?"

I felt the same way right now. What use was it getting scared? My situation was simple: I either found this man and killed him or I enjoyed my last three days of life and went to the same white room with Eve, not knowing what came after that. I decided I was going to try to find this guy. I loved my life. And if I convinced Erica I was going to die in three days I was sure she would finally sleep with me.

I got off the bed and picked up my phone to see what time it was: "7:15—Thursday, October 17." I had to get up and change or I might be late for the first period. Mr. Connor was giving a special class to prepare idiots like me for the exam on Friday. Wait, I already took that exam and didn't get shit from that class. I looked back at my phone to see if I had read the date wrong: "7:18—Thursday, October 17." I turned on the TV and looked for the date in the left hand corner: "7:19—Thursday, October 17."

I was startled by a high-pitched scream from my phone, announcing a text from Erica: "Bring my math notebook dumbass, I swear if you forget I'll…."

Now I understood how Eve intended me to stop this man before the car accident happened. She had turned back time three days.

Coincidence

"Mom?" I yelled. "Dad?"

They had left early for work, just like the Thursday before. This was happening. What was I going to do?

First, I needed to tell Erica. I needed her help. The tattoo would seem weird, but it wasn't going to convince her of the full story. I was going to need time to explain every detail. I couldn't rush her with all of it at school; between classes and other people we would be interrupted too much. My best option was to play the day out exactly like last time, forget about everything until we were alone in her house. I had seventy-two hours left to live and this was a terrible waste of eight, but I figured once I told her the truth we could make up for lost time

I grabbed Erica's notebook, ate a quick bowl of cereal and left for school. I arrived with a few minutes to spare. She was already there, just like last time, lying down in the hall outside Mr. Connor's classroom, using her backpack as a pillow. It felt so strange, reliving the past, but also empowering. Under different circumstances I would have gotten such a kick out of it.

"Come on, Erica, really? Do you know how many people walk across this floor?"

She gave me a faint groan without opening her eyes, but I interrupted her before she answered.

"No, I don't know either, but I can guess. *Anda, mi cielo, parate que se ve feo.*"

"How did you—" The bell cut her question short.

"Never mind," I said. "Let's do this."

She looked at me suspiciously. "You're kind of weird today."

"I'm always weird, love," I replied and kissed her on the cheek. "I prefer 'special' though."

She smiled. "You are."

We walked into the classroom. I took my seat and stared at the board. Mr. Connor had already drawn a perfect isosceles triangle, with a square on one of the edges identifying the right angle, and the length of one of the sides shown. Easy. I got through two other exercises with no trouble at all. How did I fail to understand any of this before? I looked at the clock and fifteen minutes had passed since the class started; one hour and fifteen to go. Mr. Connor pulled out the big guns. He started drawing circles with triangles in them and then squares with imaginary and real triangles in them and then trapezoids with triangles and random striped zones in them, asking for like three different numbers from each group of figures. I understood all of it, but I remembered I needed to act as if the last three days had never happened. I copied all the necessary info on them and left them like that. I ripped off a piece from a blank page and wrote a message to Erica. Just two words: "Hey, gorgeous."

She always sat next to me so I just put it on her desk. Erica unfolded the paper, smiled and wrote back, "What is up with you today?"

"Math makes me horny," I wrote.

She couldn't help laughing out loud and the class went silent for thirty awkward seconds.

I gave her another paper. "Seriously though, I could use some help with this."

"Fine, you can come to my place this afternoon ;)"

Getting a second look at the exercises, they really weren't that hard. But I still hated math and trigonometry. Now that I understood it and found no reasonable application for it, seeing it made me even angrier. That feeling was never going to change; if math was a physical entity I would still beat the living crap out of it.

During lunch Erica and I were talking about how bizarre it was that our history teacher looked exactly like the fat guy that stole Woody from Toy Story 2, but I wasn't paying attention to her. I kept stealing glances at my Death Signature, always reminding me that Eve was waiting and that she would get a body by Sunday, no matter what. Then I saw Samantha walking toward our table, but with some hesitance. It was a perfect opportunity.

I interrupted Erica right away. "*Mi cielo,* Samantha Vane is coming this way. She's going to tell me how terrible she is doing this semester in math and that she wants my help to study for her test on Monday." Every chance I got to show Erica that I had lived those last three days had to be taken advantage of. She had no time to respond to my unexpected interruption. Samantha reached our table and I stood up to meet her.

"Adam Lacroft," said Samantha as I hugged her.

"Samantha Vane."

"You remember."

"Of course I remember, Sammy. We made out at Sean's party, right?"

She blushed. "Not really, we just talked." That last part was addressed to Erica and then Samantha turned back to me. "I was wondering if," she said, "look, I'm really having trouble with math this semester and on Monday I have a test. And since you already saw all this last year, I was hoping you could come to my place on Sunday and help me out."

Erica looked up when she heard that.

"Sammy, I'm so sorry, but I don't think I can help. I suck at math, so I respectfully decline."

"Come on, I won't blame you for trying," she said and then bit her lower lip.

Keep it cool, Adam. You have things to do this weekend. Like pre-meditated murder and writing your will.

"I'd really love to, Sammy, but I'm busy on Sunday. Call me when you have biology, I'm good at that," I said with a wink.

She finally got the message and I watched her walk away. Damn, what a shame.

"Look, Erica, I'll explain this afternoon. You have a chemistry quiz right now." I started to run toward the exit of the cafeteria and yelled, "See you at 3:30 by my car."

At 3:30 I walked out to the parking lot and Erica was waiting for me, sitting on the hood of my car. I hurried her inside and we drove to her house in complete silence. We arrived a few minutes later.

"Mom, I'm here!" Erica shouted. "Adam gave me a ride, he came over to study."

Her mother was cleaning some dishes. She dried her hands and came to greet us. "Hi, sweetie," she said to her daughter and gave her a kiss on the cheek. Then she assaulted me with a hug. "Adam, *mi amor!*"

"Olga, how are you? It's been a while."

"It has indeed, why is that?"

"Well, Erica doesn't invite me over anymore."

"Erica!"

This time Erica was too upset to follow the joke. "Mom, look we have a big test tomorrow, you can catch up with Adam some other day." Erica walked toward the stairs and I followed right away.

As soon as she closed the door of her bedroom behind us I had second thoughts about telling her. What if she doesn't believe me? Or even worse, what if she does? Erica wasn't going to just listen and not do anything. She would want to help me find this guy. I couldn't get her involved in all of it, just so I could feel less alone. It was too dangerous. I dropped my backpack next to her desk and jumped on her large bed, wondering how I could talk myself out of telling her. She already suspected something important and she was waiting for me to explain.

"I'm really nervous about math, Erica," I started. "This is my last year, you know? What if I fail?"

"What happened at lunch?"

"Oh, that. It was just a bad joke, Erica, it didn't come out as I'd planned. I knew Samantha's class had a test on Monday. I just wanted to spook you." I turned around at the end so she couldn't see my face, otherwise she would recognize the lie. "Now let me sleep," I added as I hugged one of her pillows.

"Adam, get up! You came over to study."

I snored loudly in response.

Erica giggled and sat next to me. "Come on, Adam, be serious. You said so yourself, you need to study. I can help you. I have to go to dinner with my family in about three hours, that's all I need to get you ready, three hours."

"Erica, let it go, I'll just sleep here while you make some notes and take your notebook home when you're done."

"Okay, you win. No studying," she said as she leaned over me.

"I'm a lost cause, Erica."

"Then I can lose nothing for trying," she said softly. She stretched her thin body of top of mine.

I loved what that felt like. I was thinking of the graveyard. Of how we kissed for hours and only minutes passed. It hurt me to see that all of that was gone, that she was just teasing me to get me to study. The glow in her eyes wasn't the same. I was perfectly aware that, in this timeline, she still wasn't in love with me that way, but I didn't care.

I pulled her face against mine. If I had less than

sixty-four hours left to live I could be allowed recklessness.

She tried to push away at first, but gave in just as quickly. I held her tight, kissed her softly and paused to take refuge in the moment.

But time didn't slow down, peace-of-mind didn't show up. Their absence filled me with desperation so I kissed her more intensely, as if I was going to rip the feeling out of her. Our breathing got harder, my hands went from her back to her hips, pulling her even closer to me.

"Adam," she tried to say, but I kissed her again.

I needed the calm, the assurance that she needed me to stay alive. Erica wasn't taking me away from the nightmare and that terrified me. One of my hands went under her shirt while the other went for her belt.

"Adam, stop."

I couldn't listen. If love wasn't helping, lust might. I just wanted distraction from the damn symbol on my wrist.

Erica pushed me and yelled "Adam, stop!" She jumped off the bed, angry, fixed her belt and crossed her arms. "What the hell was that?"

I sat upright. "It's not like you don't want this."

"Not like this! Not like this, Adam. I've thought about this, I have wanted this, but—but there's something wrong with you today. This isn't you." She looked at the floor. "I think you should leave." Great. Just what I needed. I managed to screw it up with the one person that I want to spend my last living days with.

"Erica, there's something I need—I want—you to hear."

She looked over at me, waiting.

I took a deep breath. "Anta, Lucas and Crayol. They're the three biggest constellations found in your cheeks, standing for beauty, luck and crappy coloring skills. There are eight in total, all of them somewhere in the realm of your twenty-three freckles. I mapped them out on Saturday, October 19."

She had a "what are you talking about?" look on her face, so I sent back a "let me finish" look.

"Later today," I said, "you made a study guide for me, the ClearValley Senior Year Trigonometry for Dummies (Adam), thanks to which I passed the test tomorrow. On Friday, October 18, I made dinner for you at my house. I made you macaroni and cheese, just like when we were kids. After that I started to make a move on you, but I panicked so you attacked me just before you left the house. On Saturday, we went to the cemetery on the edge of the city. I can't describe how it felt being there with you."

By now she must have assumed this was some weird apology or that I was crazy, but her mood started to change.

"On the way back...."

This was the hardest part, the part where my lame apology failed and I would get kicked out of the house.

"On the way back, we crashed and I died, Erica. I know it sounds impossible, but you have to believe me."

Her expression was hard to read. She seemed surprised, but not incredulous.

"I met Death. She's not much older than we are. She offered me a deal, a way to get my life back. We signed our agreement with this." I raised my hand so she could see the little black symbol.

All the blood in her cheeks vanished when she saw it.

"Please, love, you have to believe me. Eve only—"
"Anna."
"What?"

51

Erica turned around and lifted her shirt. On the right side of her lower back was a little black symbol. A curved line with a dot on both sides of it.

"Anna, the girl in the polka-dot dress. I know her."

I Know Death Too

"How can you know who I'm talking about? She...." I sat on the edge of Erica's bed with my head buried in my hands. It all sounded so insane when I said it out loud. "I met her because I died in the crash, because she wanted to give me a second chance. If you died there too, why don't you remember those days?"

"I don't know what crash you're talking about."

"Then how can you know the girl?"

"I don't know, Adam!" Erica paced back and forth. "I don't know anything about a crash or that weekend, but I know the girl. She talks to me in a dream. I have it all the time.... Well, since you've seen her too, maybe it's a memory." Erica sat on the bed and took a deep breath.

"It was so long ago, before I met you. What would that be—nine, ten years ago? The beginning is a blur. A forest, a boat, a lake. It changes, but one thing is always the same: I drown."

She was speaking slowly. I think it was the first time she had ever told this to anyone.

"I relive it every time. The lake is never cold, or maybe I just can't tell. I'm floating there, aware of the water flooding my lungs and panic flooding my mind. The panic is worse. After the agonizing seconds in which I scream endlessly and the only reaction is the swelling of the knot in my throat, the water pulls me in deeper and I lose consciousness. I wake up relieved, rested... just like after a good night's sleep when you don't feel the urge to stay in bed longer. I sit upright and look around. It's a big room, a girl's room. Judging by the decoration it must have been a nursery once. There's a large window full of dust and the walls are a bleached-out pink. The furniture in the room is white—

a crib, a dresser—and there are shelves filled with toys and dolls, but like the walls, you can tell none of it has been touched in years.... No one has played in this room in a long time. I notice a girl sitting in front of me on the floor, but I'm busy admiring the vintage playroom. I don't know why, but something in that place makes me feel relaxed. I forget about how I got there. The girl lets me wander off in my mind then starts to talk as she combs the hair of a doll in front of her.

'These are all mine. I can't play with them anymore, but every once in a while they need some grooming,' she says.

Something about the dolls intrigues me. They are nothing like Barbie or any of the dolls I knew. They are bigger and wear old-fashioned dresses, nothing like the dolls I ever played with. 'Can I help?'

'Sure, sweetheart.' She passes me a dark-haired one whose curls are frizzy and tangled and she makes a face. 'This mess isn't going to fix itself.'

I giggle. She's kind, silly. She reminds me of my preschool teacher. We sit there, me and the girl in the black dress with white polka dots, combing the dolls, making them pretty again. She's handling a redheaded one. 'Mine is called Erica and the one you're holding is Anna,' she says.

'Erica? My name is Erica, too!'

'Well, what a coincidence. Anna is named after me.' She smiles, but it seems faked.

'I think they're both really pretty. Are they good friends?'

She never answers my question. 'You know, right now they're kind of shy, but before you arrived they were talking about something really important.'

'What were they talking about? A secret?' I gasp happily at the thought of one. In the dream I'm always

54

six, after all.

'Sort of. Erica is moving. She has to go away to another place, because something bad happened to her.'

'Can she still see her doll friends after she moves?'

'I'm afraid not. That's what they were talking about just before you arrived. Anna can help Erica stay a little longer to play with her friends, but she doesn't know if she should.' Anna's grip around the doll tightens as she says this.

I remember asking why not, but then this last part of the dream I've never understood completely. I mean, I remember. I remember the words, what she says to me, but I've never understood what she meant and her attitude toward me grows cold and bitter.

The next thing Anna says is: 'You look exactly like her.'

'Like who?'

'A friend.'

Anna's grip on the doll is no longer normal. Her fingers pierce through its body and the doll starts changing. Its hair grows gray and its white skin peels, as if rotting. 'You're too young. Not yet,' she pronounces as the doll disintegrates between her fingers.

'I want to wait until you have someone to understand why.'"

Erica grew silent and looked down at her hands.

"Is that it?" I put one of my hands on her leg. "Nothing else happened?"

"I'm not sure. I think there's more but I can't remember how we end the conversation."

A lot of this dream of hers didn't make any sense, it didn't fit with what was happening to me. Who was it that Erica looked exactly like, what was she too young for, who was the one to understand why—all these questions I would find the answers to years later, but back then the dream simply helped to support the reality of Death's participation in our affairs.

Erica rested her head on my shoulder. "She's real then... Eve, Anna, Death."

"It would appear so." I told her all about my meeting with Eve. "Hey, Erica, let me see your mark again."

She showed me her Death Signature, which, until she saw mine, she had always assumed was a birthmark. What other explanation would she have believed anyway? It was not as elaborate as mine. It was like the division sign, only cooler. Looking at it quickly it could pass as a scar, but having seen another one you could tell they came from the same artist.

"Eve told me it was the mark of our agreement. Did she ever say what yours meant?"

"No, she's never mentioned it, but I've always had a feeling that it was related to her. Does this mean I'm going to die too?"

Erica spoke with genuine concern. There's nothing in this world that I'm more allergic to. "Probably, but at least you're going to make it past Saturday."

She got mad at the joke, of course, but it was true. I had a deadline, at least she didn't.

"Come on, there has to be something, Adam. Some way you can complete the contract without killing this guy... a loophole."

It was an idea that I hadn't thought of until she suggested it, but after a flashback to the white room I dismissed it. "I wish there was, but Eve was pretty clear: I have to find the man that crashed into us and kill him."

"That's all she gave you? Not even a name?"

"Yep."

Erica got to her feet. "Okay. Let's think this

through, Adam. It seems that she can't take you herself, that she needs a middleman. If that's true, we can assume that the seventy-two hour deadline isn't precise. If she sends a regular person to kill you, it won't be until after your three days are up. And based on how she chose you, the person will probably be an inexperienced assassin. We can have a plan B, a way out in case we fail."

"How am I even supposed to find some guy I've never seen before in three days?"

"You said he had a black car, right?"

I nodded.

"Do you remember the model? License plate?"

I was embarrassed. In ten hours all I had come up with was that I should buy plastic gloves so I wouldn't leave any fingerprints. And that was because I had seen a preview of the next CSI episode before I left the house that morning. In ten minutes Erica had found a weak point in Eve's procedures, the possibility of a loophole and seemed to have a decent idea of how we could find our guy.

"Ummm... a sporty one?"

"Oh, right, I forget. I'm talking to the only boy in the world who doesn't know anything about cars. Think, Adam, the license plate."

I transported myself to the moment where I was being carried into the ambulance. The hood of the black car had exploded after impact, so the license plate was burned, but the three last characters were visible. "It ends with 'A-7-7.'"

"Well, that's something." She went to lean against the closet door and saw the dress she had hung out to wear that night. "Shit, Adam, you should get going. I have a dinner, remember? We'll figure this out tomorrow. Until then, just try to get some sleep."

She walked me to my car.

"I'm sorry, *mi cielo*. I wasn't coping with the whole thing as well as I thought."

She understood now why it was that I had been acting so weird, but she was still somewhat tense. She left after saying goodnight.

When I got home, my parents were sitting together on the living room couch. They were so happy, they always had been. I hugged them both.

"What's wrong, Adam?" my mom asked.

"Tomorrow is the trigonometry test."

They laughed.

There was no way I could convince them of what was happening to me. Erica believed the story because by some abnormal coincidence she had met Death, too. Even if my parents believed me it would only complicate things. I wouldn't be able to leave the house freely and my dad would refuse to let me hunt this man alone. If they were harmed in any way because of me I would never forgive myself. I went upstairs and turned on the computer. I needed to write some things down, in case I failed to fulfill my contract with Eve. I started with my will:

Thursday, October 17th, 2012.

I, Adam Lacroft, am writing this so that my wishes are left physically expressed to be fulfilled after my death. However informal, they are sincere. All my CDs and books go to Erica Novessel Rowan. Most of what I am was influenced by them and the rest of what I am was influenced by you, so by handing them to you, I hope there's enough of me in them to make you smile, even after I am long gone. Everything else I leave to my parents, who gave me everything to start with. I love you both so much.

You made the coolest kid on Earth once, imagine what would come out if you tried again.

I didn't want to write anything else, include anyone else. I was tired and frustrated and handsome and young and still deprived of the experience of a threesome. Lying in my bed, I thought about my simple teenage life and how it had changed so radically in three days.

Eve and her bargain were real enough, but—perhaps because it was too much to grasp—I allowed myself the feeling that things would work out in the end. There's this quote in Frankenstein, something Victor writes about calmness, shortly before his entire life was ripped to shreds, "It was a strong effort of the spirit of good; but it was ineffectual. Destiny was too potent, and her immutable laws had decreed my utter and terrible destruction."

I would one day learn that my destruction had too been decreed long before that night.

The Doctor

I groaned as I put my phone to my face. "Hello?"

"You have got to be kidding me," Erica snarled through the other side of the line. "IT'S SEVEN FORTY-FIVE. GET THE HELL OUT OF BED AND COME PICK ME UP."

"Why, good morning to you too, Miss Novessel."

She sighed in raging annoyance.

"I'm up, I'm up."

"Good. We're skipping school. I found something important you need to hear. I'm waiting for you at the bus stop near ClearVa—"

"Wait! We cannot simply skip math, we have a test."

A giggle finally slipped from Erica. "Hurry up, Adam."

I started stretching, along with the weird noises that accompany the action, when something in the black symbol on my wrist caught my eye. Instead of the three circles that surrounded the triangle when Eve first gave it to me, there were now two. The one on the left side of the triangle had vanished. Of course. The symbol was there to remind the wearer, at all times, of his current fate. It was logical then, that it should also remind me of the time that rested between me and that fate. A countdown. A cruel tease from Eve that she includes, no doubt, to make the whole affair all the more interesting. The realization brought a wry smile.

Twenty minutes later, Erica and I were sitting in a café not far from the bus stop where she had been waiting for me.

I poked her hand with a straw. "Did you get any sleep?"

"Barely. I was up all night getting a plan together."
She pulled some papers out of her bag.

I looked away from her, thinking of how, again, I
hadn't done anything useful. "Yeah, so was I."

She looked at me for a few seconds. "You didn't do
anything, did you?"

"I was asleep by nine."

I kept looking at the window next to us, pretending
not to notice that she was still staring at me, waiting for
an explanation. I gave a quick glance in her direction
and bumped into the questions in her sea-green eyes.
My answer was a guilty smile I couldn't hold back
anymore.

She laughed at it. "Eve should be getting my Death
Signature erased, not yours."

"Hey, I wrote my will."

"Do I get to burn that stupid shirt you love?"

I had this T-shirt of a badass panda holding two
guns (the coolest shirt on Earth) that Erica had
attempted several times to destroy. "Remove panda
shirt from will. Hide in vault," I wrote on the backside
of one of the papers she had put on the table. "All right,
what do we know?"

She ignored my memo concerning the well-being of
the T-shirt. "Well, the first thing I did is search for the
license plate. Since you could only remember the last
three characters, I got several hits. Fifty-six in the state,
out of which eight were vans and fourteen were trucks.
That narrowed the list to thirty-four cars, out of which
only seven are black and 'sporty.'"

"Wait. Where the hell did you find fifty-six cars that
matched the partial plate?"

"Internet."

"You're kidding."

"Nope. The wonders of technology." She spread out
some photos over the table. "Okay, so here's a picture

of all the cars, which one most resembles the one in the accident?"

"Erica, have you done this before?"

"*Maldita sea con este niño,*" she cursed impatiently. "Focus, Adam."

"I am just shocked at your efficiency." I pointed at the picture in the middle.

She picked it up and looked at the corner where she had written a number then she searched her bag for another folder. "Number five, number five, number five," she said as she browsed through it, until she found the page she was looking for and handed it to me.

It was a copy of the state registration form for the ownership of the vehicle. "Aldo Sotore," I read out loud. "Erica, did you sleep with the police station?"

She laughed. "I swear you can get this online. I had to sign up on this amateur private investigators webpage. You owe me $14.99."

Everything I needed was there: phone numbers, home address, work address, even a profile picture. Aldo was younger than I expected, he seemed like thirty-something in the photo. Slightly good looking; dark blond hair, blue eyes, nothing at all like the drunken bum Eve had implied he was. He kinda looked like Brian, from "The Fast and The Furious."

"For starters, it's unlikely that he'll be home on a Friday morning. We should try the work address first: ClearValley Hospital," Erica said.

"Excellent, my dear Holmes!"

"Elementary, my dear Watson."

As it turned out, Aldo was a doctor. Could this get any harder? Now I couldn't just wound him and leave him to die. If he was a half decent doctor he would know what to do to survive. To pull this off, I had to stay with him until I was sure he was either on the highway to hell or the stairway to heaven. That last part was up to him, though.

We arrived at the ClearValley clinical compound and I sat down while Erica went to the reception. I had never had a problem with this sort of place. I had never related them to the anxiety or sadness that most people feel. Even when its white walls and its cold air reminded me solely of Eve's waiting room, I felt nothing. Boredom at the most.

Erica came back and sat next to me.

"Mi cielo ¿Cuál es el plan?" I asked her.

"According to the receptionist," she pointed with her head at the chubby lady behind the desk, "one of Aldo's patients is in a coma and he checks on him two or three times a day. Aldo is in surgery right now, but when he finishes it's likely that he'll go see him. So what you're going to do, love," she turned to me, "is visit this poor human cabbage and talk to Aldo when he shows up. Find out at what time he is leaving today, if he will be working tomorrow, anything that can help us plan a plan."

"I think flirting with this guy will work better if you do it," I whispered.

Erica kissed me. "I'm taken."

Time didn't slow down: it ceased to exist. How can I even explain.... This is what Arctic Monkeys songs are made of.

I stood up and followed the hospital's retarded direction system to room 712. There were three beds, each separated by their respective blue curtain. The old man was in the last one and the other two were empty. I sat at his bedside and waited for Aldo there. Ten, fifteen minutes passed. Looking at this man I started wondering why he was in a coma. I mean, what did that imply? Did Eve go, "Nah, I don't feel like doing this right now, I'll deal with him tomorrow?" Or maybe he was in a queue. Supposedly, someone dies every six seconds. If that's true, how did Eve see all of them? Maybe she just attended to specific cases, like me. Either way, I felt like I should warn him about the situation.

"She's beautiful, but don't let that fool you," I whispered and thought for a second. "If you don't have anything unfinished here, I suggest you don't accept any deal she offers."

I looked to the door to see if anyone was coming, but the coast was clear. "Requiescat in pace," I said as I held his hand. A little later, Aldo entered the room.

"Oh, I'm sorry," he said when he realized I was there. "I could come back la—"

"No, don't, it's all right." I was now in character.

Aldo moved forward to see the values on the monitor and checked the bag of the IV connected to the old man's arm.

"Thank you, doctor. The nurse told me you visit him two or three times a day." I patted the man's hand. "Will he come back?"

"I still have faith in him." Aldo looked back at me. When he spoke again, his voice was bitter. "I haven't seen you around here before, though."

Crap. I looked at the face of the old man for a decent lie. "I was out of the country and I arrived yesterday." I tried to sound as unfriendly as possible. The more Aldo asked the more I would have to lie and eventually I might get tangled in my own BS. Still, I had to find out a few things. "Will you come tomorrow?"

"I'm afraid not. I... I have to take care of some things."

"Of more importance than this?"

"Of life and death," he answered dryly, with an absent-minded look. "Do you know that, since the day he was admitted, you're the only visitor he's had?"

I gulped. "I guess there's a reason for that."

"Oh, there's rarely a reason. Mostly excuses. I mean, no offense, but what the fuck have you all been doing that's so important you can't see your dying relative at least once a week?"

Well, thank you, Aldo, for that "No offense." Otherwise, that question would have been extremely hostile and offensive.

"Excuse me?" For a second, I forgot I wasn't this guy's grandson or whatever.

"You heard me. It takes a real gang of hypocrites to pay for the best medical treatment they can find and just wash their hands after signing a man over to the hospital. I bet you're all just crossing your fingers he doesn't make it through the month so you don't have to pay for November. And then you have the balls to show up and get angry because I won't see him on a Saturday morning."

From the moment I met Aldo, something about him didn't fit. Maybe it was the gap between meeting the actual him and the irresponsible asshole Eve had prepped me up to expect. Maybe that expectation allowed me to see more clearly who Aldo Sotore was. That speech, that little outburst just now, you could tell it was something he had been storing up for a while. Not for me specifically, but the way he said it, you knew it was the kind of thing that you want to say but you just shut your teeth because it might jeopardize your job or your position or your chances of success. It was the kind of thing that's fair to say, the kind that people don't like to hear.

It's funny the amount of things that only the future would be able to clarify for me. Looking back now, after everything that's happened, I can tell that Aldo wasn't pissed off because he'd had a bad day. It was not a mood swing. A man who speaks his mind is always something to admire, but Aldo spoke his mind because he knew something more, something the rest of the world did not know. He was a man that had learned the value of words and that there was no right time to say them other than when they needed to be said.

You may have noticed by now that, being young and cocky and just unbelievably bold, I grinned when things got bad. Right then, the smile across my face was ridiculous. Fuck me... this just got better and better: Aldo Sotore was a good man.

I patted the old man's shoulder. "He was the one that insisted I studied abroad. He made it possible." My eyes even got a little foggy. "He wasn't my grandfather or my uncle or my father, but I loved him."

It was time to go. I had the information I wanted. Well, part of it. All right, I didn't get shit, but I was starting to get really nervous.

Aldo stopped me when I stood up to leave. "I'll try to come tomorrow, but I can't promise anything."

I got the feeling he felt bad about what he had said, because I wasn't the hypocrite grandson he wanted to say it to.

"My name is Aldo," he said, stretching out his hand.

I shook it and was about to come up with a false name when I noticed something on his wrist. Half concealed by the white coat was a mark in the shape of a diamond, with a half-moon and a black circle on top of one of the points. An ink too similar, a symbol all too familiar.

Aldo Sotore had a Death Signature on his wrist and that only meant one thing: my death was no accident.

During the five seconds I was lost in the realization of my mind-blowing epiphany, Aldo noticed that I recognized the mark on his wrist. Before I could do anything else his fist met my face. I fell back as he pulled a syringe out of his coat pocket.

I jumped up to charge at him when I felt someone behind me. A hand held up my chin and I felt something sharp and cold against my neck.

"Drop the syringe," Erica ordered. "If I kill him, you can't fulfill your contract."

Aldo stood there, analyzing if there was any way he could get to me before Erica slashed my throat.

"I'll do it," Erica said. "I'm as deep in this as you guys."

Aldo grunted and then let the syringe fall out of his hand.

Erica kept her hold on me until we reached the hall. We ran for nearest exit.

Phantom Manor

I turned off the car and exhaled. We had stopped about thirty blocks away from the hospital, even though Aldo hadn't even chased us to the hall.

"Holy crap." My heart was still racing. "That was fucking genius, Erica."

"Expect the best and prepare for the worst."

"Oh my God, when you—"

"I know."

"And when you—"

"I know!" She reclined the seat as far as it could go and collapsed against it.

"How did you know I was in trouble?"

"I was there the whole time, behind the curtain of the first bed. I CANNOT believe you said "Requiescat in pace" out loud, I almost bit through my hand to keep from laughing."

"I couldn't miss the chance." I smiled uncomfortably. My left cheek was starting to swell up from the punch. "Son of a bitch hit me hard."

Erica gave me a small kiss as an analgesic. "Better?"

"Like new."

We were silent until our breathing finally returned to normal.

"Erica, that has to be THE most badass thing we have ever done."

"I agree," she said as she returned her seat to the normal position and put on her seatbelt. "But what now? If we found him he can find us."

I thought about it. If his Death Signature worked like mine, it showed that his deadline was tomorrow. Maybe I could hide until it passed. It didn't make sense though, why did Eve want me to kill him? I mean, he succeeded in killing me on his first attempt: why give me a second chance when Aldo had completed his contract in the first place?

"There's only one way to go from here, Erica. I need to talk to Eve."

"How?"

"I don't know, but she told me we could do it if I needed to." I turned on the car. "Let me drop you off at your house and I'll call you when I figure it out."

By the time we got to Erica's, it was about 3:00 in the afternoon.

"We should have asked Aldo for a note. Now we'll never be able to recover the exam," I said, and made a sad face.

"I don't know why you're so concerned, you were probably going to fail."

I opened her door. *"Fuera de mi carro, niña."*

She raised her eyebrow in response. "Be nice," she said as she moved in to kiss me.

"Hey, can you sleep at my place tonight? You know, to plan the hit and stuff."

"Yeah, sure." She rolled her eyes. "To plan the hit and stuff."

She kissed me goodbye and got out of the car.

On the way home I picked up a pizza and as soon as I arrived I devoured that thing like a proper fat-ass. Then I took a shower, one of the long ones, where I dissected the events of the day. I dressed, put some ice on my face and lay down on my bed. "Eve, we need to talk," I said out loud.

No answer.

"Eve, you lying snake, I'm talking to you."

Nothingness.

"My place or your place, I don't really give a damn."

I was starting to feel ridiculous so I opened my eyes.

Instead of my blue ceiling, there was a dense wall of mist. I jumped up and fell onto a poorly trimmed lawn in the middle of what used to be a garden, I guess. The bushes had been clipped into rectangles, but the flowers on them were withered. When I stood up, I could see the bushes were positioned in rows with enough space to walk between them. I couldn't see anything past the bushes in any direction, except for the silhouette of a building a few meters in front of me. I walked toward it and distinguished a sort of house. Not the typical structure of one, precisely. It was an immense, circular structure that probably stood about ten meters high. As I got closer I could see a smaller second level topped with a dome. I couldn't decide if it looked more like a ruined temple or a tiny castle. To make it even stranger, it was pink. A pink phantom manor that maybe was once bright, but now adapted itself to the dark range of tones that ruled over the entire place. The main agents of its decay appeared to be the cracks and vines that were consuming the lower level. The entrance was a massive, black gate, with an inscription on top of it. I recognized the last part:

Dinanzi a me non fuor cose create
se non etterne, e io etterno duro.
Lasciate ogne speranza, voi ch'entrate.

Nothing till I was made was made
Only eternal beings and I endure eternally
Abandon all hope, ye who enter here.

Your place it is.

I pushed the gates with some effort and they yielded. The inside of the building was somewhat more preserved. Dust and spider webs were present, but there were no weeds or roots; they were taking their time on the outside walls. The ceiling was sustained by six stone columns, spread in a three-meter radius. In the center, there was a spiral staircase that led to the second floor. The room was rich with an assortment of treasures from all over the world. Sculptures, paintings, suits of armor, maps—like an exhibition that hadn't been organized yet. As I walked through, the tips of my fingers caressed the wall. I couldn't stop admiring this place. For a moment I forgot why I was even there. I had walked through a fair portion of the room before I realized that it was divided in three. The two parts of the room nearest to the gates were pretty much the same, but the last third, opposite to the entrance, was occupied by a large, ebony bookshelf. When I say large, I mean pretty goddamn big. It must have held more than ten thousand books. I walked alongside it, inhaling the aroma of old pages, humidity and ink. God, it was beautiful. There was an old man lying in a hospital bed waiting for Death, but now I see that, apparently, she was too busy reading.

Eve's voice came from behind me. "Well, well, to what do I owe the honor?"

"I met Aldo," I said as I pulled out one of the books.

"And?"

"I noticed he had one of these bad boys," I raised my wrist so she could see the Death Signature. "And he tried to stab me with a needle."

"Oh."

"Yeah. Imagine my surprise." I turned around. "I still can't make any sense of it, though. Why did you lie to me? You knew the crash was no accident, in fact you sent him to do it. Why send me after him when he did exactly what you wanted in the first place?"

Eve was sitting down on one of her relics, a throne, with her legs crossed. She placed her hands together on her knee. "Al—"

71

"And why the hell does Erica have one too? You said she wasn't harmed, she's not supposed to be involved in any of this!"

Eve chuckled. "Does it matter, Adam? You still have to kill him. What he did or didn't do isn't any of your concern."

I glared at her. This was just a game to her, a means of entertainment when her books did not suffice. "The hell it is!" I said as I threw the book to the wall. "If you tricked him why wouldn't you trick me?"

She stood up. "So much rage, Adam, so much energy that you have inside you." She picked up the book. "Learn to control it, it does you no good. I, for one, enjoy it very much, but you will find people in the future that are not as tolerant as I am."

"Okay then, can you find it in your good nature to explain to me what the hell is going on?"

She let go of the book and it flew back, almost hitting me, to its original spot in the library. "It is only because of my good nature and the fact that I like your outbursts that I will answer some of your questions. Aldo failed in the proper completion of our agreement, I didn't trick him. I didn't trick you either, the real intentions behind the crash affected in no way the task you had to fulfill, in fact, I considered I was doing you a favor, giving you something less to be nervous about. Had you planned something a little more elaborate than walking into his workplace in the middle of day, you would have killed him without ever knowing what had caused the accident."

She sat back down on the throne and picked up an apple from a basket on the table next to her. Eve fixed her eyes on me as she took a bite. "Satisfied?"

"Not really. You still haven't explained how Erica fits into all this."

"Oh, right, the redhead. Erica drowned nine years

ago. She was on a camping trip with her family and she was left unattended in the lake. I had no hand in that. I was benevolent and generous enough to grant her some more time to live. Her death wasn't a consequence of any of this."

"Wha—"

"Choose your question well. I have things to do, Adam."

"What did Aldo do wrong?"

She flicked a speck of dust off of her dress. "Many things, Adam, there's no such thing as a saint."

"I mean, what did he do wrong when he killed me? You said he didn't complete his contract successfully. You don't want someone messing up your plans twice in the same week, right? A little advice won't kill me," I turned around to browse through her books once more. "You have that part pretty much covered."

She stood up and walked slowly. She slid between me and the bookshelf, leaving me nowhere else to look but her smile.

Goddamn, that smile.

My rage wasn't gone, just dormant. It was just lulled to sleep by her melodious voice and her hypnotic gaze. It's hard to hate something you're inexplicably attracted to.

She put her hand behind my neck, pulled me closer and whispered in my ear, "You'll manage."

Our foreheads pressed together, she was well within kissing range and I was having trouble avoiding the urge. I breathed deeply, considering the many reasons why it was wrong. She's a supernatural entity, Adam. Then again, that would imply supernatural sex. Hell yeah. No man, get a grip. This is fucked up beyond words, she's just toying with me.

Eve smiled again, to let me know she understood everything that was going on in my mind and ended my struggle by putting the fruit in her hand between us.

"Apple?" she offered.

"That didn't go too well for the last Adam."

Eve rolled her eyes. "You don't believe in such fairytales, do you?"

"You're here, aren't you?"

"Adam, sweetie, I'm made of something much stronger than faith and poetry."

"Lies?"

She fluttered her lady eyelashes and looked at me with her eyes full of death.

"Hatred."

And just like that, I was back in my room again, lying in my bed with a pack of ice on my face. Hatred? Hatred for whom? My curiosity for what Eve could have meant by that vanished quickly though. I had enough to think about. I still had to kill Aldo Sotore and now I wanted to kill him even less. Even after learning that he crashed into my car on purpose, I still couldn't blame him for it. Eve was responsible for the sick games she was playing with our lives. And for her to talk about us like that, as if she was doing us a goddamn favor....

I was determined to find a solution in which Death would not get her way. I sat on the floor, crossed my legs and concentrated on recalling every word Eve had ever said. A fragment of our first meeting had played itself in my mind: "'I'm Death, I know if you're going to die or not. But your reasoning certainly amused me. There have been cases where people come this far and are brought back, especially with technology these days. But you're not one of them.'"

To die is by definition "the cessation of all biological functions that sustain a living organism." What if I manage to induce Aldo into that state for a short time and then bring him back? My contract stated that I had to kill him: it said nothing against reviving him. And no matter what his contract was, it would end as well the instant he died. I would spare myself the murder charge and at the same time fuck with Eve a little for making me miss the math exam. Cocky bitch, if she wanted to play with me I was going to give her a hell of a game.

I grabbed the papers from my desk and dialed the phone number written on the form. He had one day left too; he couldn't afford the luxury of sparing any viable options. At the very least, I was sure he would want to listen. After the first two rings, he answered.

"Hello?"

"Aldo Sotore, my name is Adam Lacroft. We met at the hospital this morning."

"So you're the kid." He sighed. "What do you want?"

"I want to get this thing off my wrist, don't you?"

"Of course I do, but you know as well as I that there is only one way to make that happe—"

"That's why I'm calling you. I have an idea, so we can both make it."

"Kid, we either fulfill our contracts with Helena or die."

"Hear me out. Do you hate her?"

There was silence on the other side, as if he wasn't expecting that question.

"More than anything in the world," Aldo said.

"The enemy of my enemy is my friend and my enemy is Death. Look, I found a loophole in the contract."

"I'm listening," Aldo said.

King's Game

Erica arrived at my house at seven, just like last time. Not as fancy, but just as beautiful. Blue jeans, a white tank top and over it a red and black checkered shirt, with the sleeves rolled up. My dad came out and said hi to her, like last time, and sent her up. As soon as she entered the room I put my hands around her neck and pushed my face against hers repeatedly, giving her a wave of gay/cute pecks until she needed the space to breathe. She shoved me away, giggling, and blushed at the sudden act of excessive affection. Erica let her backpack fall next to my bed and asked me if I had managed to find a way to talk to Eve. I told her about my second meeting with Eve, focusing more on the description of her apparent residence, delighted at the memory of it.

Eve, I had concluded, was some sort of hipster that thought it cool to adorn her place with literary references such as inscribing on her gates the poem from the Divine Comedy in the very same fashion that it is inscribed over the Gates of Hell. The medieval maps and suits of armor, the ebony bookcase, the art collection hanging inside the massive chapel, works from as far back as the Renaissance to as recent as Surrealism, the constant allusions to Catholic mythology—all of these things made me feel sure that Eve had not always been this spirit of demise. The very definition of the composition of her being, hatred, given by no one other than herself, was evidence of feeling. The poisonous flirting with which she addressed me, the childlike caprice that preceded her arrangements with the living, her subjects... Eve had not always been Death. I was convinced that she had been human once, a woman, to make it worse and that she was one day either condemned or surrendered to the office she practiced now. It would appear that, being bored by it, she dedicated herself to her own amusement at the expense of these complex and delicate "second chances" she so generously handed out.

I told all this to Erica, but I omitted the part in which I wanted to ravage Eve inside a timeless museum. It would have been too weird to explain. *"Ojos que no ven, corazón que no siente."*

More important than that, though, was the plan that I had come up with. It was clever and when I told Erica about it she admitted that she would have never thought of it. I gave Erica a transcription of my conversation with Aldo. She was impressed that I convinced Aldo to comply, as the plan involved considerably more risks for him than for me. But at the end, he had agreed and we had arranged that we would meet tomorrow afternoon, at his house, to end all of this once and for all.

"Now, as to why you're here, Erica," I said holding her hands. "We have to acknowledge the fact that there is still a high chance that I might die tomorrow."

"Adam, don't say that."

"I'm scared too, love. But it's a reality and I have to face it. I never thought I would have to say this, but I want you to know that if I had one night left to live, and it's possible that I do, I would like to spend it with only one person."

Erica looked into my eyes, waiting for her name.

"Oscar Wilde." I looked away from her. "Or Kaya Scodelario. I can never make up my mind. Wilde would provide me with the most interesting conversation I could ever hope to engage in. But Kaya, she's the most gorgeous thing alive, she has to be mine in this life. Hell, we could work something out. I don't know about

Kaya, but I don't think Wilde would disagree to an indecent propo—"

Erica smacked me in the head.

"But, but, but," I grabbed her hands so she wouldn't hit me again, "let me finish. One is dead and the other is dating some British guy and nothing beats a British guy, not even me. So, I'll have to settle with you, Erica Novessel Rowan, the girl that I will always love, no matter how bad her Spanish is."

"*Imbécil*. I hope you do find her one day and I hope she turns you down."

"Oh!" I gasped in exaggerated pain. "Have you no heart?" I moved in to kiss her.

"It belongs to you, inexplicably." She kissed me back.

Right about then was when the drinking started. Erica foresaw that that night was going to be all about forgetting my imminent doom for a while and she thought the aid of stimulants would be necessary. Since the breakdown I'd had on Thursday, I had been coping with the situation decently, or so I liked to think.

I objected to the alcohol at first. Erica alone supplied me with every vice and rush I could crave. Also, waking up with a hangover the next day was not wise, much less welcomed. Despite this, one "pretty please" and a few flutters of her eyelashes was enough to have me drinking from the bottle.

"By Zeus," I coughed. "What the fuck is this, Erica?"

"Oh my God, you're such a girl, it's just vodka."

"I mean, what brand?"

"Let me see," she said as she turned the bottle to read the label.

I stood next to her so I could see it too. The label was silver and simply said "Bodka" in gold letters. We looked at it for about a minute, as if waiting for the ingredient board or the alcohol percentage to appear. Nope, just "Bodka."

"Well," I said as I grabbed the bottle and walked toward the window, "nothing to do here."

"NOO! I paid good money for it," she said as she tried to snatch it out of my hands.

"To whom?" I laughed, incredulous at the rescue attempt of this godforsaken liquid. "A pedophile rapist? A medical research team? The fat guy from Toy Story 2?"

I could think of a few other possibilities, but I was incapacitated by one of those hysterical laughter attacks in which you think you're going to faint from the lack of oxygen. So was Erica, but even in that state she was still trying to protect her precious investment as if she had distilled the thing herself. I had to support myself on the frame of the window, the bottle in peril as the strength fled from my hand while I gasped for stability.

"We-we-we," Erica snorted into laughter again, taking me with her. "W-we," she gasped deeply, "we have to, we have to drink it, Adam, at least half."

Erica's face was red and there were tears in her eyes.

"Drink this? *Mi cielo, ¿me estas jodiendo*?" The fact that she insisted on swallowing poison still amazed me. "Drink this? Erica: This is what you pour on an open wound to prevent an infection. This is what experimental jet-fuel is made of. If you stab a chupacabra in the eye, this is what comes out. This is what the CIA used to brainwash Soviet soldiers captured in Vietnam. This is what Lewis Carroll was on when he wrote Alice in Wonderland. In 1978 the World Health Organization branded this as a cause for a terminal systematic disease. Grey Goose has spent decades trying to synthesize the perfect vodka and this is one of the failed, surviving prototypes. In the classified inventory taken from the Roswell UFO incident in 1947, this bottle was among the possessions recovered from the alleged crash site."

I stopped to breathe, but before I could continue Erica succumbed to the hysterical laughter attack once more. "How do you even come up with all this shit?" she said in a weakened voice.

"It's all true, love."

"Okay, we'll make a deal. Two more gulps each and then you can do what you want with it."

"All right," I said as I handed her the bottle. "Ladies first."

She took a huge gulp. She didn't defend the thing so ardently in vain; she was willing to enjoy every drop. But regardless of her unconditional love for Satan's tequila, the taste was exceptionally bad. She swallowed what she could and ran toward the window to spit the rest out, but not surprisingly she missed and spat the thing right on my wall.

"What the hell, love," I groaned.

She fell to the floor, giggling, demonstrating that the abilities of Bodka were not to be trifled with. I grabbed the bottle, took a huge gulp and felt the bitter pang immediately. I ran to the window and spat on the other side of the wall. I ended up on the floor next to her, unable to speak for the next three minutes out of sheer abdominal pain. When we recovered from the Bodka's siege, she walked straight to my closet and started searching through my clothes. I knew right away what she was looking for.

"It's not there." I put my hands behind my head and stretched out my legs. "I hid it, as a precaution. It hurts me to see that my fears were justified."

She pulled out one of the drawers and turned it upside down. "Where is the panda shirt, Adam?"

"Whyyy? I spared the radioactive substance you

brought into my home."

"It has to go, Adam. I need to destroy it," she said as she looked under my bed. Then she moved on to the drawers of my desk.

It wasn't there either, but she found something else that lit up her face. "I'll play you for it."

"My Xbox is dead, remember?" I said as I crawled to her. Then I realized she was holding a black leather briefcase that I had not opened in some years.

It was a fever we once had, when we outgrew the movie marathons. We had played every time she came over, to determine who was the smartest. A king's game once, now sadly dubbed a nerd's pastime by the mindless youth of most of my generation and those adjacent: chess. I had a beautiful, fancy set that my father had bought in Paris when he still had all his hair.

"You're on."

We set it up on the floor, in the free space next to my bed. Erica was good at it. Under normal circumstances accepting the challenge would have meant the certain destruction of the shirt. But these were no normal circumstances since Bodka was in her system. I had to seize the opportunity. By risking this one time I could settle the dispute of the panda shirt forever. Erica's evident tipsiness gave me confidence that this game was mine to win.

She made the first move, the pawn in front of the left rook. I copied it. She made the same move with the pawn in front of the right rook. I copied it as well. Erica referred to my moves angrily as "cheap strategy." I didn't care. I would cheat my way to victory if I had to. I kept the same stance for a while, replicating her every play, annoying her, hoping that rage would add up to the blinding factors that would make her lose the game. But I knew I couldn't keep it up for the whole match and the moment I made my first independent move the tension leveled up. It was as if Erica had sobered up momentarily, just to see me fall. I lost my queen in a dumb move and she gave me that evil smile of hers while she took it, letting me know that no matter how drunk I thought she was, she would never let me win. However, she lost a bishop for it and I noticed that as I picked it up from the board she took off one of her shoes.

The game went on similarly, with me losing important pieces for equal or less significant ones. She took my rook for a pawn, my knight for a bishop, my other rook for nothing, because I left it unguarded. I looked at the pieces she held captive in despair. I was running out of important players, my horizontal and vertical offense limited by the defeat of my beloved rooks. I was looking at the pretty black figures, neatly lined by her side, when I realized something important. Next to her little chess cemetery were her shoes, her socks, her earrings and her necklace. I was so focused on whatever she was planning on the board that I had not noticed the pattern she was following during the match. Now that I saw perfectly what she was doing and it was then when I knew that I was going to lose the game. This kind of strategy was unprecedented in the history of chess.

For every piece she lost removed a piece of clothing.

How does that help her? Well, the question answers itself when I'm thinking, "Why the hell is she taking off her clothes?" instead of thinking, "Hey, that knight has nowhere to go." My heart started beating faster. Erica had a wicked mind, and how I loved her for it.

Discretely, I took off my shoes, my socks, my watch and my necklace, to compensate for the pieces I had lost. I should have taken off more, but I figured Erica wouldn't say anything yet.

The game carried on, more slowly now that we were both aware of the conditions under which we were playing. Motivated by these very same, I finally made a kick-ass move and took her queen.

"Wow." Erica kneeled. "Nice." She started unbuttoning her shirt. Locking her eyes on mine, she wanted to make sure I forgot every decent play to follow up with. Her hands moved calmly, for every second she spent undressing herself damaged significantly my chances of victory. When all the buttons were undone she puffed her chest forward as she slipped out of the checkered garment and put it on top of her shoes.

"Your move," she whispered.

"Check," I said as I put my remaining knight in range of her king, taking the poor pawn defending the spot.

Erica moved her bishop to the defense of its king. She would have lost it, but she didn't care anymore. She kneeled again and her fingers started undoing her jeans, the sound of the zipper going down being the final move of the match and declaring Erica arrogantly and unanimously the victor.

Fuck this, I surrender.

I threw the chessboard across the room. Erica felt the same impulse and jumped at me, pinning me to the floor. She kissed me impatiently, as if I was going to slip away from her at any minute, intensely, as if she needed to verify that every single part of my skin was real.

It was as though the fear for my preservation was shared by her just as fiercely as if it was her own that was at stake. The effects of the alcohol in my body were upstaged when I realized that just knowing that she needed me to live, whether I liked or not, set the climax of ecstasy that my being could sustain.

Half naked and welded to each other, we managed to find my bed. All the feelings between us stored for years, the patient longing and the hostage desire, all of it detonated at that very moment and the result for something so complicated as love was as simple as instinctive. I buried my head in my favorite part of the female anatomy: her neck, the spot just below the left ear. I could smell her warmth, taste her happiness, feel her scent.

Having completed that step, having captured the raw essence of Erica Novessel Rowan, we resumed the carnage.

Elsewhere

I felt the cold utensils beneath my palm and my awareness of them surprised me. I picked the fork up and balanced it carefully between my two index fingers so I could take a better look at it. The handle was intricately engraved with a pattern like that of vines crawling up a tree, of veins tied around a limb. The fork was made of pure silver. Eve giggled from across the table at my examination.

"That is called a fork. It is for eating," she said as she grabbed her own fork and mimicked the action of putting food in her mouth with it.

"It's no ordinary fork. Well, it's a fork all right, but I don't know…. It's opulent and elegant. One of a kind. Nowadays things are never both. In most cases, opulence is the very opposite of elegance."

I looked at the restaurant around us: the tables, the plates, the cloths, the glasses, the people and their clothes. Everything had that same feeling, emitted that same sense of class. There was electric lighting, but all the tables had two or three candles as a complement. The waiters walked between the tables as unnoticed as if they were part of the building. The room was large and the tables were separated from each other enough to allow privacy, but just the right distance to make everyone's conversation a smooth background track.

I tried to recall how I had gotten there, but there was a gap in my memory.

Right on cue, Eve answered my train of thought that she supposedly could not hear. "I wanted to apologize for earlier."

Ah. Now this started to make more sense.

"Is this a dream? Or your place?"

It felt too real to be a dream, but then again, her

place never had any people.

"It's a dream," she said. "You've seen my place, sweetie, I'm of more eccentric tastes. It's your dream, but as long as you and I have business pending I can pop in. Shape *it* a little bit."

"Okay. So, are you going to tell me the truth about Aldo?"

"No. I'm just apologizing for being rude about it."

Why does she want to talk to me then? I mean, it can't possibly be because she is afraid of what I think of her. Because she cares whether I was mad at her or not.

"Apology accepted, anything else?"

If I had blinked I would have missed it, but I was entirely focused on her and I saw it: a spasm in her expression that lasted only a fraction of a second. A spasm she had tried to hide. My disinterest in whatever she had to say seemed to have hurt her, as though she cared. If she does care what I think of her, or at least how I treat her, why is she making me go through all this?

"I thought," she said, "I could make it up to you. Give you something that, in your reality, is impossible to obtain." She smiled. "Do you know where we are?"

"In my dream, what's so special about it?"

"Well, technically. But I told you, as long as I'm here it's no ordinary dream. We are in the Café Royal, Regent Street, London, 1895."

I scratched the tablecloth as my fists closed in surprise. With that movement, everything on the table skittered a few inches toward me. I scanned the whole room again. I had never seen any of it or anyone in it before. It was not a creation of my mind. My dream was the medium, but I felt the spotless white silk between my fingers and understood that it was real, as real as it had once been *in* that specific moment in time.

Eve grinned proudly at the effect once I had realized what her gift was. "The book you picked out from my library this afternoon was The Importance of Being Earnest. Out of all the books in there you went directly to that one, so I had a hunch that you might be a fan."

How could she know that? I mean sure, Wilde was an easy guess given that I picked that book out of hundreds, but how could she possibly know my fascination with life in that specific part of the nineteenth century? It scared me and excited me at the same time, just how much I was interested in her and that, apparently, the interest was mutual. How could she be so thoughtful, to the point of recreating an entire era for me, but also cold enough to allow the possible destruction of my life just for her amusement?

"I thought you might like a night in this world you've only read about, but if you'd rather go back to bed," she said as she raised one hand.

"Wait." I stopped her before she snapped her fingers and stared directly into her black eyes.

Eve has no obligation to do any of this, nothing to gain out of it. The look on her face when I was about to reject her offer was a slip-up, genuine. The threat of sending me back, a bluff. Eve was lonely, but I could not use that against her. She had nothing to gain except my company, my admiration, my happiness, for the duration of the dream at least. Likewise, all that could come out of this for me was her company, her admiration, her happiness, for the duration of the dream. Despite everything that had happened since I met her, I decided to grant her the chance to make me feel these things and for her to feel them from me. A date with Death.

"Dinner and a movie?" I said.

This time she didn't seem to care if I saw or not how she felt. She smiled eagerly. "In a way. Dinner, and the movie will remain a surprise for now. Before that though, we need to go get you a nice suit. You're a little underdressed, Adam."

I had not noticed that, all this time, I had been wearing my Mario Bros pajamas. I was a little embarrassed, but no one around us seemed to mind, they kept about their business as if we were not even there. Eve was wearing a fancier version of her normal black dress with white polka dots.

I tucked my shirt in, as if that was going to make a difference. "Couldn't you have changed that before you brought me here?"

"When I cross someone over they come with whatever was on them, I don't control that."

"Really?" I leaned across the table to whisper the next question. "So what if I had been naked?"

She took a sip from a glass of wine in front of her, leaned closer and whispered back, "We would have gone… elsewhere."

I know it seems a little hard to grasp, the fact that I switched off so easily. But that's always been in me, the ability, or more like the capacity, to assess opportunities that would appear controversial. I believe in the coexistence of non-conflicting interests. I was planning on tricking Eve tomorrow and never seeing her again. Eve knew that she was directly responsible for whatever demise fell upon me. That did not change the fact that we could enjoy a nice conversation. The limits of our relationship did not blur because of it. Truth be told, as the night went on I started to feel a little sorry for her. The more I saw of her and the more we talked about anything other than my contract, the more I realized the conditions of life that she was subject to. The perks that came with her god-like state of being did not outweigh the disadvantages.

After dinner we took a cab to Victorian London's

finest tailor shop. As the carriage bounced through the streets I looked at all the buildings in wonder, but Eve didn't seem to share my fascination. If anything, she viewed them with a hint of disdain. She seemed to know everything about history, art, film, literature, geography and biology and that was *l*ogical, she had more than enough time to read and learn. More than that, she had firsthand knowledge of a good deal of what she talked about. After all, in a way, she had been there. Being immortal, she had seen the sights, witnessed the events, met the people. But what does that matter? She doesn't appear to have any friends or family. What good is it if she can share it with no one? When you cannot have that, but you cannot die either… why bother living? Everything that is important in life is unavailable to her because of the nature and the responsibility of her trade. So what is it that drives her?

"Eve?"

"Look, we're here."

The shop was managed by a quaint old man. He acted strangely, like everyone in the dream. They all ignored me and avoided her. I wondered if they were real, as in people who existed back then, or if they were part of the landscape of Eve's extremely accurate recreation of then.

The old man took my measurements and showed me to a fitting room with a wooden block in the middle for me to stand on and three mirrors around it for me to see how I looked. Eve sat in a chair and laughed from time to time at the awkwardness with which I moved in this scenery where I did not belong. The old man came *i*n with a dark, striped, gray, three-piece suit and a high-collared shirt and hung them between two of the mirrors. The fabric was very thick, but it was comfortable. I was going to take off my shirt, but I stopped.

Eve rolled her eyes. "Oh, all right," she said and walked out of the fitting room.

I put on the pants and the shirt and asked her to come back in to help me with the vest.

"Eve?"

"Shh! Hold still," she said as she buttoned the vest.

"Eve?"

"My, my." She circled me. "Clive, you haven't lost your touch."

The old tailor stepped outside the fitting room and Eve followed.

"But I think one size smaller will do… and some cologne."

"Yes, Miss Valero."

"DO NOT CALL ME BY THAT NAME," she hissed at him.

"I-I am sorry, Miss Vale—I meant no disrespect."

"I damn sure hope not. You're done for the night, Clive."

Eve came back in the room and I pretended that I did not hear any of the conversation. "Now, about the 'movie,'" she said as she finished grooming me and hurried me outside. "There's been a lot of talk about a new play showing in the St. James Theatre, a comedy."

"Eve?"

"What, Adam? What is it?"

I thought the question over again for a second. "Why are you, I mean, how—You were human once, weren't you?"

She turned *h*er face away without giving me an answer.

"Were you?"

"Some time ago."

"Then why—how can you do this?"

The question, I know, was ambiguous, but she knew exactly what I meant by i*t*. My question was at first,

"Why are you Death?" but after thinking about it, what puzzled me most was, "How can you be Death?" How, after knowing life, after knowing love, can you endure it? How can you survive it?

"How can I do this? How can I willingly be Death?"

Her tone puzzled me. It was threatening, as she had been offended by my concern. Still, all that came out of me was a mechanical "yes."

"How could anyone choose this? To live alone as an empty body in a void where there is nothing but time and the knowledge that you are in fact dead, dead forever?" Her voice grew angrier. "The irony of having only one task: to claim and collect every life that passes on in this world, without so much as an ounce of that life rubbing off on to you?"

She laughed and everyone in the dream stopped moving.

"You think Death is the cruelest thing one can ever go through. But you see, Adam, you are young, you have seen *n*othing yet. You think Death is cruel because Life has not shown you what she is capable of." She grabbed my hand and put it against her chest so I could feel her there, but notice the lack of a pulse. "I am this, I do this, because Life is the real antagonist. You think Death gives me emptiness; she gives me peace. Death has been an example to me; Life made an example out of me. Death has been kind and she has provided me with the means to teach Life a lesson, to exact revenge on the fruits of her *i*njustice."

Eve had never before lost her temper in front of me like that. It shocked me. Every word she said had cost her tremendous effort because of the duality of emotions that they evoked. Anger, sadness and joy were all there to certify that she was not lying, but that she did not believe everything she was saying. To me, the whole speech, the dream, how close she had let me

91

in... it was all a cry for help.

"So what happens once you've taught the lesson? Once you have finished what Death has allowed you to do?"

She turned her back to me. If she was human she would have been crying. "I don't know. I'll find out someday, though."

She did not say so, but I was sure that I was the only person she had talked to like this since she had stopped being alive. What happened tomorrow then, if I died and never wanted to speak to her again? What happened tomorrow if I completed my contract and returned to life and never saw her again?

I wanted to know what happened after tomorrow to her. I had the feeling that for some reason she had felt that I was different, that I had turned out to be a speck of matter in her void, her emptiness.

"And tomorrow? What happens after tomorrow?"

She understood, of course, everything I really meant to ask. Nothing had to happen necessarily; she could leave the signature on me and I could carry on with my life during the day and rub some of my life into her during the night.

"We could be friends," I said.

She seemed conflicted by the proposal, but the larger purpose she had been talking about overruled my offer. In a way, I was asking her to choose between Life and Death. I learned later that I had not been the first to do so. On both occasions she chose Death.

She declined with a sad smile. "Life is for the living, Adam."

Loophole

At the time, I hadn't stopped to think about what had happened to Aldo that led to the signing of his contract with Eve. I sympathized with the fact that he was being forced to do it, but I didn't really care. It was months later that I would achieve a better understanding of how Eve had come into his life and how much suffering she had brought upon him. I had never imagined that his contract was so demanding. His involved several murders and the price to pay if he failed wasn't his life alone.

When we had talked over the phone, the plan Aldo and I had agreed upon was this: he had to create the conditions in his body that would result in his death when I administered the final component, in the form of an injection or a pill. After that happened, I would bring him back with a shock or an adrenaline shot. All the science of it I left in his responsibility, I merely came up with the concept of a loophole that would benefit us both. It was a complicated plan and to attempt it without Aldo's consent would have proved impossible. He had been reluctant at first, because it sounded good enough in theory but the truth is that the part he played in it involved much higher risks than mine. One cause of concern was the margin of error for a procedure like that. The other was the possibility that I might betray him and leave him there to die. "I really don't want to kill you, Aldo" I had told him. "I'm too pretty to go to jail."

We had decided to meet in his apartment at 3:00 p.m. I got the feeling we were both stretching out the little time we had left before one of us died, but the stated reason was that Aldo would need to work his morning shift in the hospital to pick up the materials he needed to carry on with the idea I had proposed.

On that morning, Saturday, I opened my eyes to find a gorgeous redhead clinging onto my chest. I caressed Erica's naked back, naively thinking that it was all going to be over by nightfall.

"Rise and shine, sunshine." I kissed Erica on the forehead.

It took her a few seconds because she refused to wake up completely. I poked her head until she finally decided to answer, but all that came out was an unintelligible mumble.

"It's about ten," I said.

Erica mumbled something again, her face still stuck in a pillow.

"Yes, I will make you breakfast, you fat-ass."

"Mmmhmm-mmm, mmmh?"

"Why, yes, I would very much enjoy morning sex right now."

The suggestion gave her enough energy to lift her head. "I said, 'Go get started, I'm going to take a shower.'"

"I see no obstruction to the morning sex part."

"It depends on what you prepare for breakfast." She stood up, wrapped in my bed covers, and stopped at the door. "Are your parents home?"

"I'm not sure. MOM? DAD? ERICA IS NAKED SO STAY IN YO—"

Erica jumped back and punched me. "What the hell, Adam!"

I picked up a pillow to use it as a shield. "Relax, love. They're never home on Sunday mornings, they go jogging or something."

"IT'S ALL RIGHT," my dad yelled from the bottom floor, "I WAS JUST ABOUT TO LEAVE."

We froze for a few seconds, but then I couldn't help laughing.

"If Aldo doesn't kill you today," Erica said, her face as red as it could get, "I will."

"Wait a second, there's something I haven't told you about today."

"What is it?"

"I'm not going to tell you until you lose the attitude," I said as I crossed my arms.

Erica huffed, but sat down next to me on the bed. Erica's mood was volatile when she was sleepy, but I knew how to handle it. I pulled her against me so I could kiss her. My free hand relieved her of the bed covers and I positioned myself on top of her.

"Adam," she said as she pulled me back by my hair so I couldn't reach her lips, "we have to get up."

"You're right," I said, grinding my body against hers, "let's stop then."

Erica loved to be teased. She was about to make another objection when I pressed her harder and as a result she gasped in my ear. All comments after that were either inarticulate or of a more intimate nature.

We had woken up at 10:00. We got out of the bed at 10:48.

I started cooking lunch at 11:00 when Erica walked into the kitchen. Lunch was... delayed until 11:31. We finished eating at 12:00. The kitchen table, however, remained... occupied until 12:22.

I went to take a shower. Erica had forgotten something in the bathroom.

We were dressed by 1:00.

"We'd better leave right now," I said. "Aldo lives about an hour from here."

Erica nodded and then started undoing her belt.

So much for leaving right now.

I remember the time frame of that morning so specifically because of the process it took to leave the house. The willpower that was demanded of us when all we wanted to do was stay home and share body heat all day. Looking at her eyes whenever I said, "We really need to get going" and reading "I don't care, I'm happy like this. Let's stay like this."

We walked outside and before we got in the car I told her to close her eyes and stretch out her arms. There was something I wanted to give to her before we left. The ultimate sacrifice I ever made for a woman, I gently placed the panda shirt in her hands.

"Will you do me the honor?"

She rolled her eyes when she saw what she was holding. "Just this one time, Adam," she said as she took her other shirt off and put mine on.

It was somewhere around 4:00 when we finally got there. We arrived at the street he had given us, but I wasn't sure which house was his.

"Call him," Erica said.

"Are you crazy? I'm not going to call him."

"Why not?"

"What do you mean 'why?' 'Hi Aldo, I'm almost here to kill you, but I'm a little lost, could you step out for a second and show me where I can park?'"

"I hadn't thought about the parking."

"I'm not calling him," I said again.

"I don't see what the big deal—look! There it is, number 52!"

I parked across the street and we walked to his door. As soon as Erica knocked I ran to the car.

"Adam!" she hissed. "Get back here!"

"I just realized the number was 51, not 52."

Erica's face turned red and she ran to hide behind a bush.

I started laughing. "I'm joking, it's number 52." I leaned against the car. "Oh my God, you should have seen your face."

"What the fuck, Adam?"

She was kinda mad, but she started snickering. Our fooling around was cut short when Aldo opened the door. We froze on the spot.

"You're late," were his first words.

"You live on the edge of the world," I said as entered the porch.

Erica hurried behind me and elbowed me. I turned and whispered to her, *"¿Qué? Esta mierda queda en el quinto coño."*

She stepped on my foot and then stretched out her hand toward Aldo. "Hi, I'm Erica."

"Aldo," he said, and shook it.

We all stood there for a second, acknowledging the awkwardness of the appointment.

"I think you should let me punch you in the face," I said to Aldo, "Seeing as, you know, you punched me in the face."

Erica sighed and massaged the middle of her forehead with one hand.

Aldo looked at me and then at her. "Is he serious?"

"Of course I'm serious. You hit my good side."

"Adam, shut up."

"Seriously: you punched a minor square in the face. Didn't you feel weird after that?"

"Can we come in?" Erica asked.

I found her dismissal of my argumentation extremely disrespectful.

Aldo simply nodded and turned his back on us, leaving the door open so we would follow behind him.

We all sat down in his living room and Aldo began to explain to us what it was, medically speaking, that we were going to do. Well, to Erica, because he preferred that she listened, that she be the one endowed with the instructions of the process and not me, because he assumed I was more likely to screw it up. I was offended of course, it was me who was going to do it, it was my responsibility, but more than that, I was offended because this pretentious jerk apparently assumed that I was not as intellectually capable as Erica.

When I objected he gave me an incredulous look and said, "Your first words here were: 'I think you should let me punch you in the face because you hit my good side.'"

"But you did hit my good side."

Erica resorted to that burning gaze of hers that guaranteed that one day she would be an excellent mother. "Adam, *callate, mierda.*"

Fine then. I crossed my arms and sat away from them in protest, but still listening to the lecture. "The brain," Aldo explained, "can survive up to three minutes without oxygen, no longer." He told us that he had spent a good deal of time thinking of the way he would approach his death and resurrection, for there was more than one. Quite a few, in fact. He had looked for the most likely to succeed, but more important, one that would result in virtually no permanent damage to his body. From that criterion he had discarded heart attacks via the disruption of the sodium-phosphate pump or through hypotension caused by a morphine overdose. A defibrillator would have served for the resurrection purposes, but there was no predicting how well or how fast his system would recover from the shock. He had chosen something that all doctors were used to and therefore knew how to handle well: an overdose of sedatives, more than 300mg of Propofol and 10mg of Milazolan, to be exact.

Aldo had set up a single mattress in his living room, with a monitor on the left that would, *valga la redundancia*, monitor body temperature, heart rate, blood pressure and oxygen levels in the blood. He attached the device to his index finger and showed us what the normal vital signs were like and explained how they would change after I injected the anesthesia. On the left of the bed there was a tray with the compounds that were to induce his death and bring about his revival. We would use the little vial of Laxenate to counteract the reactions caused by the overdose, but only after the monitor had pronounced him dead.

In short, he would lie down, insert an IV line in his arm through which I would administer everything, I would then supply the poison and when the oxygen in his blood was less than 20% and the line representing his heartbeat flat, he would be brain dead and only then could I give him the antidote and start pumping oxygen back into his lungs. Slowly, he would come back to life and after his vitals were back to normal he would be but asleep, and would wake up in an hour or so.

Before the point of no return he reminded me, "It's extremely important that you keep calm and follow the instructions to the letter." He sighed a final time, still unsure if he could trust me with his life. "If you do this right, when I wake up I'll let you punch me in the face."

With that, I pushed the liquid into his body.

The normal numbers, the evidence of health, lingered for some time after he was unconscious, but eventually they started decreasing and alarmingly, in a matter of seconds, they dropped to the limits Aldo had set.

Something had gone wrong.

"Erica, what's happening?"

"How the hell should I know?" she yelled, kneeling next to the body.

"You were the one he explained this whole thing to!"

"You know the same crap he told me, asshole!"

The beeping on the monitor was now going off, uninterrupted.

"Shoot him the other vial!" Erica said as she grabbed the air pump and put the tube in his mouth.

I injected the Laxenate and watched the monitor, waiting for the numbers to rise. "It's back to 30%, but the heartbeat is the same."

"He said not to panic. Give him 30 seconds and if they're not changing by then, we try CPR."

I started counting out loud. "1, 2, 3, 4, 5, 6, 7, come on, Aldo, 10, 11, 12, 13, 14, 15, 16, 17, 18, 19, 20, 21." His vitals remained the same.

Fuck it. I put my hands where Erica pointed and pressed down hard. 1, 2, 3, again! 1, 2, 3, again! "Don't let her win, Aldo, she can't win!" I screamed as I pressed again and with a convulsion Aldo's heart came back to life.

Erica and I sighed as the monitor changed from an annoying wail to a reassuring tempo.

I held my wrist up to see the Death Signature. It started to fade, to evaporate out of my skin, but before the figure could become unrecognizable I felt a pulse. The ink repositioned itself back into the original symbol, clutching onto my skin with its last whim of life, clearer and brighter than ever.

After one last look at the little triangle with its three half-moons, I fell next to Aldo, unconscious.

Godfather Death

"Adam Lacroft." Eve's voice was cold.

The thick white mist was there again and it didn't let me see anything past Eve or the ground. I lay on the dark, withering grass, which I assumed was part of the garden that surrounded her house, though I could not see the mansion. I could hear a muffled roar coming from somewhere below us. Eve was sitting in a beach chair in front of me. The chair, like everything here, wherever this was, was in some level of decay. The webbing was frayed and the frame was rusty.

"Eve." I winced as I stood up. "Why am I here?"

I've mentioned before that Eve has this way of talking, that no matter the subject she has the ability to make the conversation a familiar one. When she had explained my contract it made me think of a charming manager that was selling me a product. Right now I saw her as a boss about to fire an employee. Her beautiful jawline was as rigid as porcelain.

"I'm having a hard time figuring—no, that's not it. Deciding. Yes, I'm having a hard time deciding the best way to make sure that what I say to you next sticks in your head and you never forget it."

Her girly voice and gorgeous face usually gave her an air of innocence, but right now they were not hiding the fact that she was furious, perfectly capable of exploding if I set her off with an unwanted gesture or comment.

"I want to tell you a story." Lady-like, Eve crossed her legs and smoothed out the wrinkles in her dress. "A poor man had twelve children and was forced to work night and day to give them even bread. When therefore the thirteenth came into the world, he knew not what to do in his trouble, but ran out into the great highway and resolved to ask the first person whom he met to be its godfather.

The first to meet him was the good God, who already knew what filled the man's heart and said to him, 'Poor man, I pity you. I will hold your child at its christening, and will take charge of it and make it happy on Earth.'

The man asked, 'Who are you?'

'I am God.'

'Then I do not desire to have you for a godfather,' said the man. 'You give to the rich, and leave the poor to hunger.'

The man turned therefore away from the Lord, and went farther.

Then the Devil came to him and said, 'If you will take me as a godfather for your child, I will give him gold in plenty and all the joys of the world as well.'

The man asked, 'Who are you?'

'I am the Devil.'

'Then I do not desire to have you for a godfather,' said the man. 'You deceive men and lead them astray.'

The man went onwards and then came Death, limping up to him on withered legs, and said, 'Take me as godfather.'

The man asked, 'Who are you?'

'I am Death, and I make all equal.'

'Then,' said the man, 'you are the right one. You take the rich as well as the poor without distinction. You shall be its godfather.'

Death answered, 'I will make your child rich and famous, for he who has me for a friend can lack nothing.'

The man said, 'Next Sunday is the christening, be there at the right time.'

Death appeared as he had promised, and stood godfather quite in the usual way. When the boy had grown up, his godfather one day appeared and bade him go with him.

He led the young man forth into a forest, and showed him an herb which grew there and said, 'Now you shall receive your godfather's present. I will make you a celebrated physician. When you are called to a patient, I will always appear to you. If I stand by the head of the sick man, you may say with confidence that you will make him well again, and if you give him this herb he will recover. But if I stand by the patient's feet, he is mine, and you must say that all remedies are in vain, and that no physician in the world could save him. But beware of using the herb against my will, or it might fare ill with you.'

It was not long before the youth was the most famous physician in the whole world. He had only to look at the patient and he knew his condition at once: whether he would recover, or would perish. So they said of the physician and from far and wide people came to him, sent for him when they had anyone ill, and gave him so much money that he soon became a rich man. Now it so happened that the king became ill, and the physician was summoned. But when he came to the bed, Death was standing by the feet of the sick man, and the herb did not grow which could save him. 'If I could but cheat Death for once,' thought the physician. 'He is sure to take it ill, but as I am his godson I will risk that he will shut one eye.' The physician therefore took up the sick man and laid him the other way, so that now Death was standing by his head. Then he gave the king some of the herbs, and he recovered and grew healthy again.

Death came to the physician, looking very black and angry, threatened him with his finger and said, 'You have betrayed me. This time I will pardon it, as you are my godson, but if you venture it again it will cost you your neck, for I myself will take you away.'

Soon afterward, a severe illness befell the king's daughter. She was his only child and he wept day and night, so that he began to lose the sight of his eyes and it led him to make known that whosoever rescued her from death should be her husband and inherit the crown. When the physician came to the sick girl's bed, he saw Death by her feet. He ought to have remembered the warning given by his godfather, but he was infatuated by the great beauty of the king's daughter and the happiness of becoming her husband. He did not see that Death was casting angry glances at him and threatening him with his withered fist. The physician picked up the sick girl and placed her head where her feet had lain. Then he gave her some of the herb, and instantly her cheeks flushed red, and life stirred afresh in her.

When Death saw that for a second time his own property had been misused he said, 'All is over with you, and now the lot falls on you.' With his ice-cold hand, he seized his godson so firmly that he could not resist and led him into a cave below the earth.

There the physician saw thousands and thousands of candles burning in countless rows, some large, some medium-sized, others small. Every instant some were extinguished and others again burnt up, so that the flames seemed to leap hither and thither in perpetual change.

'See,' said Death, 'these are the lights of men's lives. The large ones belong to children, the medium-sized ones to married people in their prime, the little ones belong to old people; but children and young folks likewise have often only a tiny candle.'

'Show me the light of my life,' said the physician, thinking that it would be still very tall.

Death pointed to a little end which was just

threatening to go out, and said, 'Behold, it is there.'

'Ah, dear godfather,' said the horrified physician, 'light a new one. Do it for love of me, that I may enjoy my life, be king, and the husband of the king's beautiful daughter.'

'I cannot,' answered Death. 'One must go out before a new one is lighted.'

'Then place the old one on a new one so that it will go on burning when the old one has come to an end,' pleaded the physician.

Death behaved as if he were going to fulfill his godson's wish and took hold of his godson's frail candle. But as Death desired to revenge himself, he purposely made a mistake. The little candle fell down and was extinguished. Immediately the physician fell on the ground and now he himself was in the hands of Death."

The way Eve had told the story, it made me live it. In her eyes, I had crossed her in the same way that the physician had crossed his godfather. I realized a little too late the consequences of that act. Fear surged up my back. "Where are you going with this?"

"Where I'm going with this, Adam, is that I gave you a second chance. I offered you an honest opportunity and you went and pulled this little stunt. I thought you smarter than that." She stood up from the chair and stopped in front of me. I could feel something forcing me to bend my head to look her in the eyes. "Where I'm getting at, Adam, is that I can't be escaped, tricked or persuaded without paying a price. And you, Adam, will spend every day of the rest of your miserable life paying for the day you dared to try to cheat Death."

"I KILLED Aldo Sotore. I couldn't care less about how you feel. We had a deal and I came through with my part, so get this damn thing off my wrist."

Her face did not display the wrath I was expecting. It didn't show much of anything, actually. She simply stretched out her hand, asking for mine.

I looked into her big black eyes, unable to move. I tried, I was trying with all my strength to run away from her, to break from her gaze, but it was impossible. Wherever we were it was her domain and I was sure that while we were there Eve could do anything she wanted. She took my right arm gently and stroked the back of my wrist, where the Death Signature was, with her thumb. Eve looked at my eyes once more, waiting for fear, regret or tears. Probably all three, but all she found in them was a proud, silent 'fuck you.'

And that finally set her off.

I let out a scream as she pierced my wrist with her fingers. They dug in easily all the way to the bone, where she stopped to let me know that this was my final opportunity to ask for mercy. I kneeled involuntarily, disoriented from the pain. I felt something warm and thick sliding down my arm, but I couldn't even raise my head to see my hand. I could only see the little black drops that fell on the ground. Ink, not blood, was flowing out of my body and with it the cursed tattoo on my skin. I told myself it wasn't real, that she only wanted to torture me for as long as she could before she sent me back. With a final effort I coughed and asked her, "Are we done?"

She smiled. Then she crushed what was left of my wrist.

I had never experienced anything more excruciating and I doubted that I ever would. A few more seconds and I would have fainted, but Eve kept me up with her heel against my chest. The mist had cleared enough so that I could make out the silhouette of her castle behind her. The roar below us grew louder and I realized we were right on the edge, thirty meters above a rocky shore.

"You're free to go," Eve said, and pushed me off the cliff.

I woke up with a gasp, drenched in sweat. Erica was sitting next to me.

"We need to leave," I said.

"What happened, Adam? Did it work?"

"I'll explain later. Right now we just need to get out of here," I said as I grabbed her by the hand and pulled her toward the door.

I turned as I opened it, to take one last look at Aldo. He remained on the floor, his chest swelling up and down peacefully. Aldo was alive and my Death Signature was gone. The loophole had worked. But this wasn't over. Not at all.

At 8:32 p.m.

"Adam, please, tell me. What did Eve say?"

"It's fine, love. Eve just wanted to see me to get this thing off my wrist."

"If it's fine, why are you shaking?"

"It's just cold."

"It's not fucking cold. What happened with Eve?"

"ERICA, Jesus Christ, I don't want to talk about it right now, okay?"

I immediately felt bad about exploding on her like that. Erica didn't get mad though, she gave me a slow kiss on the cheek and whispered in my ear that everything was going to be okay.

I turned on the car and she leaned against the door and fell asleep. Not long after we got on the freeway, we passed the entrance of the graveyard we had visited on Saturday. It was going to be a while before we got back home.

I had spent almost four hours in Aldo's house, more than half of that time unconscious, spiritually in some messed up dimension that Eve calls home. Why did she let me go? Was she incapable of taking a life herself, like Erica had assumed? Eve was able to take me from this world whenever she felt like it, could she really not keep me?

If there was some sort of supernatural principle that kept Eve from taking me because I had won my life back, then this was the end of it. If she could keep me though, if letting me go was a choice, then there must have been something far stronger behind her decision and I had much more reason to be concerned. Eve had made clear she wasn't done with me. In the way she saw it, my life was still hers and she would return sooner or later to claim it.

The sun reached its curfew and the sky turned black. The road was completely empty for miles ahead, something that was normal for a freeway this far away from the city, but on this particular night there was nothing ordinary about it. I recognized the very same intersection where Aldo had crashed into us last Saturday. The same two spotlights appeared on my left, right on cue. Eve didn't waste any time.

This time I reacted faster though, I pushed the accelerator down, speeding up the car just enough to avoid the fatal blow, but not the crash. The front of the other car exploded on impact and flipped my car. It rolled over twice, beating me against the wheel and the door. When the car stopped moving we were hanging upside down, tied up by the seatbelts.

"Erica! Are you ok?"

"What happened?"

"Are you hurt?"

"My arm," she groaned.

"Hold on," I said as I unlocked my seatbelt.

I fell onto the roof of the car on my shoulder. Ignoring the sting of broken glass, I crawled out through the window. My legs crumbled when I tried to stand, but I managed to limp to the other side of the car. Everything hurt like hell, I felt as if my limbs were on fire. Blood from a cut on my forehead was making it hard to see, but all I could think about was getting Erica to safety. I opened the passenger's door and kneeled next to her.

"*Mi cielo*, I need you to unbuckle your seatbelt. I'll catch you."

She undid the belt and I grunted as I tried to keep her from falling, but the strain of her weight was too much for me in that state. At least I managed to keep her from hitting her head. Erica crawled out of the car and we sat on the road for a few seconds to catch our breath. Then she stood up, but I couldn't. I had experienced this same thing the first time I met Eve, when she transported me in and out of the highway. But for a few seconds only, it was much easier to endure. Erica said she was okay and apart from the hurt arm I didn't see any major injuries.

"Who the hell crashed into us this time?" asked Erica.

"That's a good question," I said as I looked at the wreckage. "It's Aldo's car, but... the loophole worked. Why would he do this? It couldn't have been him, but whoever it was, there was no way he could have survived that. His engine exploded the second he hit us."

Erica took out her phone, but it was smashed. "We need to find a phone. And we should probably get away from here."

I pressed against my arm to slow down the bleeding. "Give me a sec, love. Christ, this hurts."

Erica gasped. "Adam!"

I sat upright to look at whatever she was looking at and the image made me loose what little blood was still flowing through my face.

Aldo was walking toward us, with a gun in his hand.

"No," I squealed. For the first time in the last three days I was sure I was about to die. "Your heart stopped. I felt you die!" The anguish in my voice was pathetic, but I had completed my contract. Why did Eve have these rules if she didn't follow them?

Aldo stopped a few feet in front of us. His eyes were red. "Kid...." He sighed; his armed hand was trembling.

I stood up and raised my arm so he would see that the Death Signature was gone. "The loophole worked, look at my hand!"

"I know it worked."

"Wait, then why are you doing this?"

"Helena, Eve, whatever her goddamn name is, wasn't happy with this."

"Eve threatened me too, but—"

"Look, before it was just my own life that was at stake, but I have a daughter. Julie is just nine years old."

"Aldo, please," I said.

I couldn't think of anything more to say, but Aldo was addressing himself now rather than me. "She's all that's left of my wife," he said with a breaking voice, "I can't lose Julie."

"I-I'll take care of her. I'll marry Erica, I'll start working!"

Erica finally reacted and jumped up next to me. "We'll make sure she gets everything she needs. I promise!"

"If I don't finish this she's never going to stop hunting Julie." Aldo was crying. "I've sacrificed too much already. I can't stop now."

"Just hold on, let me come up with something!"

"I'm sorry, kid, I really tried to find another way but there isn't one." He took a deep breath and raised the gun.

"ALDO, GODDAMN IT!" I screamed.

He pulled the trigger, twice.

I stretched my hand out, involuntarily, as I heard the gunshots. I heard the bullets whizz by me. I heard the hollow beat as the lead hit her body. I heard the splat of her blood and the thud as Erica fell to the ground.

"WHAT THE H—" but he was gone.

I kneeled next to Erica and put her head on my leg.

"What the hell?" I said, uncertain of who in the world had the answer to that question. He didn't shoot me, he didn't miss me. "Why the fuck did he shoot you?"

"Shit, I was thinking about it this morning, but I didn't want to worry you. I-I think maybe I've been the target all along."

"What? No, Aldo tried to kill me before, at the hospital."

"Did he? He punched you when he could have used that syringe he had. Think about it. Eve said Aldo had messed something up, right? Maybe the first time we crashed, he was supposed to kill me, but you died instead." She coughed, she was having trouble breathing. "Maybe that's why Eve gave you your contract."

"This isn't a favor," Eve had said, "it's an exchange and there are terms that have to be met, otherwise I won't come through with my part." When I had asked her about what Aldo had done wrong she had responded "Aldo failed in the proper completion of our agreement, I didn't trick him." Erica was right, Aldo was never after me.

"But why you?" I asked Erica.

"That I don't know either, love."

No… but Aldo did. As soon as Erica recovered I would find him and ask him myself. I searched my pockets for my phone, but it must have had fallen out during the crash.

"I'm going to call an ambulance," I said, but Erica stopped me.

"They didn't get here in time last time, remember?" She coughed.

"You're not going to die, Erica."

"I am. Eve isn't going to let me out of this for a second time. I can feel it."

"No. You're going to be fine, just let me go get som—"

"Just stay with me till it's done, Adam," she said as

112

she grabbed my shirt to make sure I didn't get up.

I surrendered as I caressed her cheeks. "How will I pass math without you?"

She smiled. "You'll find some other pretty girl to tutor you."

A tear slid down my face and fell on her chest, now red with her blood. "You stained the Panda shirt," I pointed out.

She giggled, the last one I would ever hear and that broke me.

"Adam, please promise me—"

"Promise you that I won't do anything stupid? How can I promise you that when you are the only thing in my life that makes sense? *Mi amor, mi cielo, mi vida,* how can I promise you anything knowing that if you die tonight everything I am dies with you?"

She smiled through her tears. "That was a pretty good line," she snuffled. "Kiss me."

As I kissed Erica the last inch of her life escaped her body. I felt her lips grow soft and I rested my forehead on hers, sobbing. She would never kiss me again. The little girl with the strawberry-ice cream, the one that I grew up with, the thing that I loved most in this world, was taken from me.

At 8:32 p.m. Erica died in my arms.

Broken

I skimmed through the newspaper, its gray, simple, characters bearing a colorful description of the bleak condition of the present—everything a consequence of the past and an obstacle for the future. I knew I'd find it: the story was big enough to make some profit for the paper, but not small enough to allow them to ignore it in search of a more appealing catastrophe. They had mentioned the crash before, but today on page four, bullied into a small box by other events that were deemed of the world's utmost concern and urgency, was our story.

The police have been puzzled this last week by the death of high school student Erica Novessel in what first appeared to be an accident in the outskirts of the city, within a few miles of ClearValley Cemetery. The autopsy revealed, however, two bullets lodged inside her chest, turning the case into a murder, for which no suspects have yet been declared. The vehicles of Doctor Aldo Sotore and the Lacroft family have both been placed on the scene, but the whereabouts of Dr. Sotore and Adam Lacroft, who was presumed to be driving the car that belonged to his family, are still unknown. The young girl's funeral is scheduled for Thursday. Her family and her friends....

At the end, there were a few lines that the author of the article had dedicated to our families, in an expression of pain and sympathy. Well, that just means the world to me, Mr. Journalist.

Reading the newspaper, all of it, I found myself hating every word and everything that helped to make it. That newspaper, the supposed authority of human communication, the herald of its events and its "truths" was the factual evidence of the world's hypocrisy. Its stupidity… its lack of humanity manifested in its entire infrastructure, absent in religion, politics and society. I found myself hating this world, disgusted by the things that people do. Why thank YOU, Mr. Journalist, for taking the time to give a fuck. I'm sure you have not slept in days thinking about how two families were destroyed.

I drove out to see Erica's grave a week after the funeral. It was autumn then and the cemetery was gray, courtesy of the storm clouds that darkened the graves and the branches of the half-dead trees. There was nothing beautiful or heroic about it anymore: it was grim and macabre and selfish. Her tombstone was somewhere around the northeastern corner and walking there it didn't mean anything, but I froze when I found the grave. Behind it was the large sycamore tree. Close by was the lake and the columbarium. I clenched my fists.

She was buried in the same spot where we had spent the afternoon together.

It was too much of a coincidence. Out of all the land in the place, it had to be there. I walked up to the tombstone and my legs weakened with every step until I fell to my knees, close enough to touch the engraving. Here lies Erica Novessel Rowan, beloved daughter and friend. Taken before her time, she will remain in our memory forever. 1994-2012.

"Mi cielo," I started, but I was silenced by the knot swelling in my throat. I took a deep breath and tried again.

"Hi, love…. I shouldn't hang around here for too long, so I'll go straight to the point. I want you to know I'm sorry. I want to apologize, not for what I have done, but for what I am going to do. I don't know if you can see me or hear me wherever you are, but I just thought I should tell you I'm not going to keep my promise to not do anything stupid. What I am going to do will be the exact opposite: it will be planned and thought through. That is what makes it worse. I'm going after Aldo. I know you wouldn't want me to, but it's just not fair. Wherever he is, he is alive with his daughter. Wherever you are, it's new and it's different and it's probably a better place. Where I am, there is our school, my room, my car, the chess set, The Ring, your family, my family, pianos.... Where I am is your grave. I was dealt the worst hand in all of this and that's why I don't expect you to understand. You can miss me just as much as I miss you, but don't think for a second that we are suffering equally. Please try to grasp the fact that you got to leave and that I got to stay."

I stopped, imagining Erica's reproach. If she could have, she would have scolded me for every word. The knot was too much now and I put a hand over my mouth to muffle a sob. The urge to just cry there and die was uncontrollable, but I could not die just yet. I would have to be content with crying. "Love, I'm pretty sure I told you... I hope I let you know, but how could you? How could you ever really know what you mean to me? What you are to me. I miss you, I want you, I love you, but now all that's left of you is a memory, a memory I will avenge."

The timeline was clear to me. When we crashed the first time, it wasn't an accident like Eve said it was. Aldo had killed me instead of Erica. Eve must have gotten upset and sent me after him as punishment. What I didn't understand is why she insisted on Aldo being Erica's killer and why she wanted to kill Erica so desperately.

I wiped my tears and steadied myself. With great effort, I managed to get up and walk away.

On the path back to the entrance of the cemetery

there was a dead crow. The corpse made me think: Is there an animal embodiment for Death? No. Humans are the only species sick enough to have someone that wanted to take the job.

We all have the same potential for good as we have for evil. But I know better now… it's not about what you can be, it's about what you want to be and we are all driven by the selfish thought of our own happiness.

I would have married Erica and we would have adopted Julie. We could have been a family. Aldo could have made that happen, but he decided to kill my happiness in exchange for his own. When he did, he cracked something in me and from that day I was forever broken. There was nothing left to me in this world, except finding Aldo and breaking him, too.

Fifty-eight days had passed since the last time I had seen Aldo. Threatened and double-crossed by Death, he had taken his daughter and fled that very day. He had moved toward the coast, three states away. My guess was that he didn't have the money to procure fake passports and vanish into a different continent after stepping off a private jet. His little blonde handicap had probably prevented him from engaging with shady smugglers. Still, Aldo had made it difficult. I had run into several dead ends, but I finally found him.

It was a shitty apartment. The fact that it was cheap and small made it clear that he was trying to keep a low profile. I tricked the landlord into giving me a set of keys and waited until Aldo left. I opened the door and made my way through the kitchen and the living room in eight or nine silent steps. Julie, his happiness—or what remained of it—was asleep on his bed. I sat on a chair next to her and I craved the peacefulness with which she slept as I pulled out the gun from my jacket, screwed on the silencer and let the gun rest on my lap.

I wondered what these months had been like for Aldo. The running, the uncertainty. Knowing I was out there, but not knowing if I had forgiven him, not knowing if I had killed myself or if I had simply failed to find him. What was it like for him, believing desperately in any of these paths, in any path that never crossed his again?

I heard the jingling of a set of keys approaching the apartment door. He closed the door silently and I counted the eight steps that were needed to reach the only bedroom in the apartment. As I felt him come in I stretched out my arm, pointing the barrel at Julie's head.

"I spared your life," Aldo said.

"It means little, compared to what you took," I answered without turning my head. Julie's sleep had not been affected in the slightest. "You would have done us both a big favor if you had let me die."

"Stop pointing that gun at my daughter, Adam," he said, taking a step forward.

I flicked off the safety. "Move another inch, Aldo…. Do it, so I can get this over with."

He stood still, refusing to lose his ground, so I encouraged him again by pulling back the hammer. Just the sound, the clicking of the mechanisms of the gun, served as a bigger threat than anything I could say. The next click would be the trigger.

"Did she send you?" he said.

"No," I scoffed. "But that didn't stop you."

He couldn't look me in the eye anymore and stared at the floor.

"Why her? Why did Eve want Erica dead?"

"Do you know what happened to my wife, Adam?"

"Why should I give a damn?"

"You should give a damn because, under Death's command, I killed her." He leaned against the wall and slid down softly to the ground, as if he had lost the strength to stand.

Since he had first mentioned her on the day of the second crash I had given little thought to his wife and what had happened to her.

Aldo let out a sigh. "Natalie had a diamond shaped symbol on her ankle, half of which was blackened in. When I asked her about it, she swore she had no idea where it had come from. The only thing she said was that she thought it was somehow related to the dreams. The conversations with a girl in a black and white polka-dot dress that she had almost every week. I really did not know what to make of them, not that they represented any danger back then. The only thing that was ever odd was how real she assured me they were, the feeling that they were not dreams, but memories."

A chill ran up my back.

"But the dreams started escalating. Natalie's screams would pierce the night, 'I WON'T DO IT, I WON'T DO IT!' and after waking up she would succumb to violent episodes of depression, refusing to explain to me what she had seen. Sometimes she simply mumbled, 'They're not dreams, Aldo, she's real,' over and over. The morning after she would pretend it had never happened or that she didn't remember. The only reasonable explanation that I could come up with was that Natalie suffered from some degree of schizophrenia, so I tried to treat it. We went to shrinks, we got her medicine, but it never helped, she only got worse."

"'The goddamn pills are not going to do anything, Aldo,' she said one day. 'The only way I can stop the dreams is by doing what she's asking me to do.'

'What is she asking you to do?'

She never answered that question. She just kissed me desperately. 'I love you; I will never do it, okay?

119

Never.' But one night a bad feeling woke me up and I found her pointing a gun, the same gun that killed your girl, at her head.

'Natalie, what are you doing?'

'She wants me to kill you, Aldo.'

'Natalie, give me the gun.'

'If I don't do it, she will. Then she'll kill me and then Julie will be all alone,' she sobbed desperately.

'Honey, we'll work out a way, just give me the gun.'

Natalie was about to hand over the gun when Death possessed her again. 'No, no, no! I CAN'T, I CAN'T!' and then she pointed it at me."

My hand started trembling. I flicked the safety of the gun back on.

Aldo didn't seem to notice. "And then I was in the white room with the girl in the polka-dot dress. You know what it's like, kid, you've met her. Very calmly and very concisely, she explained to me who she was and what was happening to my wife. Natalie had had a near-death experience before she met me and because of that Death could interact with her when she pleased. She had begun tormenting Natalie with the threat that if she did not kill me, she would take us both and leave our Julie to fend for herself. In a few seconds, I lived what Natalie had been enduring all this time and I too grasped the terrible fact that this girl was real. I realized that either one of us killed the other or we would both die. It was too much for Natalie; she loved me, and she loved Julie."

This was the first time that I began to grasp Eve's macabre nature and the magnitude of the evil of which she was capable of. "So you killed her?"

"I told Death that I would do whatever she asked me to as long as she let my wife and my daughter alone, but that was not what she had in mind. She asked me to kill Natalie and a girl, and in exchange she would leave Julie and let me live to take care of her."

"So you killed your own wife?"

"I saved her!" he yelled. "I chose to sacrifice MY happiness, MY sanity, the love of MY life so that she would not have to. I was to live the rest of my life broken so she could die in once piece." Aldo rested his head against the wall and sighed. "So, to answer your question, kid, as to why she wanted your girlfriend dead, I don't know. I don't even know why she wanted Natalie dead. Don't you think I asked her? Don't you think I needed a reason, too? She only answered, 'They're not the first and they won't be the last.' Sometimes she would go on this rant about how everything she was doing was because we all deserved it and the only objective, Adam, that she ever hinted and that I perceived, the only intention behind all these contracts was to cause our raw and pure suffering. Yours, mine, Julie's, Erica's and Natalie's."

"But why them? So the bitch has a grudge on mankind. Why Erica, why Natalie specifically?"

"I don't know! And I don't know how knowing would make it any better. She simply gave me a date and a place in which I would have the opportunity, but before that you showed up to see one of my patients. When I saw your signature and the fact that you recognized mine, I knew Eve, as you call her, had altered something. I decided to try what you proposed to me because I didn't want to be an instrument of hers; I didn't want to cause the destruction of someone else that was inflicted upon me. I wanted revenge against her and what you proposed was the closest thing available. And it did work, kid, but she played dirty once more and I did what I had to do to save my little girl."

Aldo's explanation renewed and justified my hatred

for Eve. Aldo had killed Erica, he had pulled the trigger, not Eve, and I still hated him for it... but I would not be an accessory to Eve anymore.

"I'm sorry about Natalie," I said.

"I'm sorry about Erica," he replied.

Of Questions, Anger, Violence and Speed

Four years had passed since Erica's death. The sea roared beneath the ridge and the clouds hung black above it. Eve had probably been expecting me for some time, but that day was the day I was coming in.

There's a reason this highway is one of the *l*oneliest in the country. Seventy-five meters is a long way down, even in a heavy car, and about fifty cars each year were devoured by the rocks that rested hungry at the bottom. The pavement stretching ahead of me was stained occasionally with the tire marks of the unfortunate victims that fueled the highway's reputation. Why anyone had the idea that this road would ever serve as a reliable connection between Eastern and Western Europe eluded me, but for what I wanted it for it was perfect.

The questions had never left me. Why Aldo's wife? What was her connection with Erica?

Natalie and Erica had been targeted. They had been harassed by Eve in a similar manner and their death had involved the deliberate suffering of a third party, of those closest to them. That much must have been planned before it was put into action. The anger because of that never left me. It was what fueled me. There was no one to answer for what had happened to me, to them. I had no idea of how I could hurt the person responsible for all of it and that ate me away. Revenge wasn't going to bring Erica back, but the fact that I could not have it left me impotent. There was no way to drain the pain inside me. There was no moving forward.

I used to think Eve had done it for her own twisted entertainment, but that really didn't seem enough of *a* reason for what had happened to us, to them. Aldo had satisfied himself by deciding the reason wasn't important, but the only explanation that made sense to me was that, for some reason, Eve had a list. A list of people she wanted to kill. The thought had encouraged me, because it meant that there was still a slim chance of fixing things. It would cost me, though. I would have to show Eve that I was willing to do anything to get Erica back. I would have to offer Eve not something that she did not have, but a power which she thought only herself possessed: the power of Death.

I turned on the car and got back on the road. As I pressed the accelerator and the car picked up speed, memories of the past four years broke loose.

65km/h.

I remembered the time I had started down this path.

It was late at night. I was returning to the abandoned building where I had been squatting since I had last seen Aldo. I had entered the alley and was walking to the door at the end when a woman who was leaning against the wall moved to block my path.

"Hey pretty boy, want to take me for a ride?" she said as she flashed her breasts.

"No," I said, and I pushed her aside.

One of her hands went to my crotch and the other on my shoulder, to pin me against the wall. "For you, I'll make a special offer."

Before I could refuse again, two guys sprouted from the darkness of the alley behind the woman. One placed himself on my right and the other closed in on my left, with a gun pointed at my temple.

"You give me everything you have and we don't kill you," said the woman.

I breathed anxiously as I looked at the two guys. The one on my right didn't seem to be armed.

"See that door over there?" I said as I pointed with my chin to the rusty excuse for a door. "That's where I live, what makes you think I have a dollar on me?"

"Plenty of dealers 'round here," said the one on the right.

The one on the left poked my head with his gun. "And you don't look like much of a junkie, but I guess you could say we wanted to take a 'stab in the dark.'"

The woman laughed and a knife gleamed in her hand.

I had run into them deliberately, but that didn't mean I wasn't scared. My knees were weak, my hands were shaking and my heart was close to exploding. How can I do this? They had nothing to do with what happened to me.

Then I heard Eve chuckle inside my head.

I knew wherever she was, she was laughing at my weakness. At the fact that I wasn't strong enough to do what was necessary.

She was wrong.

"I have my wallet in my back pocket, but that's it," I said.

I tightened my grip around the handle of the gun tucked in my pants and in one swift move I pulled it out and put it against the chest of the guy on my left. With my left hand I grabbed the armed hand that was pointed at my head and moved it forward. I pulled the trigger and the other guy pulled the trigger as a reflex, shooting his partner. They both fell, *d*ead, at the same time. The woman screamed as I pressed the smoking barrel of my gun against her chest and choked as I put my fingers around her throat.

"Shut up. You're going to meet a girl. Black dress, black eyes, beautiful smile." I put the barrel against her forehead. "Tell her that Adam Lacroft is coming to take back what she stole from him."

I pulled the trigger.

I couldn't loosen my hand from around her throat. If anything, my grip was even harder. It had happened so fast. It was as if I had been possessed by someone else. I let her go and I fell to my knees... Jesus Christ, I had killed three people. It felt horrible, but it was not harder than losing Erica. It was not harder than knowing she was gone.

If I was to endure more of this though, I would need some training. I decided to join the army.

90km/h.

"Lacroft, take the back door."

I signaled Cass to stay close. We were advised to expect resistance and though the house was in complete silence, I could feel them there. We reached the main hall and we were just a few steps away from one of the rooms when I stopped. I heard the creaking of the wood floor following our steps. I heard the creaking upstairs giving away the position of the rest of the team, but not the creaking of the people we were looking for. They knew we were coming. The silence and the snap of a loading mechanism were enough giveaways. I threw myself to the floor as the bullets blazed through the walls. Cass wasn't as perceptive and because of that he was hit. The shooting stopped and the thud of my partner's body hitting the floor acted as a lure. I heard the men behind the wall walking to the door that connected their room with the main hall. As they turned the knob I opened fire and someone grunted. I jumped up, kicked the door open and ran into the room. Two men were dead on the floor and I shot the third one as he attempted to escape through the window.

"Clear!" called Nate from upstairs.

"Clear! But Cass is dead. Is the target secure?" I

asked as I walked upstairs.

"Yeah, we got him." Nate knelt down, confirming the lack of pulse. "Chief is dead, too. You're next *in* command."

I walked into the main room of the second level and examined the wooden crates full of weapons stolen from our armory. Three men sat handcuffed in the middle of the room.

"Nate, get HQ to confirm the target and check out the other two."

Nate took pictures of the men and sent them out.

Our target smiled. "I love the charade you guys put on. You know I'll give them a few names and I'll be out in six months."

I crouched to look him in the eyes. "I hope so. Maybe next time there will be a 'dead or alive' option."

Nate walked back into the room. "Okay, we have confirmation. An extraction team is on its way. There is one thing, though."

"What's that?"

"These two other guys, they're just hired guns. HQ says they're not interested."

"What does that mean?"

Nate sighed. He waved his palm in front of his neck and did a cracking sound with his mouth.

"Are you serious?"

He nodded.

I thought about it. I looked at the two other men again. You don't really get to meditate about it when you're in the middle of a gunfight, so it doesn't bother you that much. But at that moment, when they gave me the chance to think about it... it didn't feel natural. It didn't feel wrong, but I just remembered that, regardless of what they had done, there was something alive breathing in front of me. That didn't stop Eve though, so it wasn't going to stop me.

"Say goodbye to your pals," I said as I pulled my gun out of its holster. "They're not coming with us."

130km/h

I preferred to go alone, but one night Nate had decided to tag along. I had warned him not to.

It was a cheap, noisy bar. We didn't have many weekends off, but when we did we were allowed to go sightseeing. I preferred to be alone because I liked looking for trouble and I usually found it. Bar fights are easy to start, and easier to put away. The only thing I found hard was knowing when to stop. Sometimes I settled a fight that had nothing to do with me. Sometimes I stood up for women that were being mistreated. One time I beat the shit out of a guy for simply being a dick. I didn't care much for a reason— all I wanted was the violence.

I dissed Nate constantly, but he seemed to like me. I liked the fact that he never asked me about my past. He never asked about anyone's past. He thought anything that couldn't be changed was irrelevant. He was right in a way. There's nothing you can do about the past, but his mistake was thinking that it did not apply to the future as well.

We sat at the bar and ordered two drinks.

"Shitty bar," he said.

"Cheap."

"Is this really where you like to spend your only days off?"

I took a gulp. "Yes."

"Why?"

A man was walking behind us with six beer bottles in his hands. I stood up and bumped against him on purpose.

The bottles fell to the floor and he yelled at me.

These people couldn't speak English, but he made it clear that it wasn't something nice.

"Adam, what the hell was that!"

"You asked me why I come here, Nate."

Two other men walked up to us. One pulled out a knife.

I finished my drink. "I come for the thrills."

The man with the knife lunged at me. I grabbed his armed hand and deflected the attack then I smashed my glass on the back of his head. I went for the second one and I landed a punch that threw him over a table. The guy whose beers I had knocked down tackled me and we fell to the ground. He managed to hit me a few times, but I flipped us over and punched him in the nose.

Blood splattered on my face.

I hit him harder.

I heard Aldo crying.

I hit him harder.

I heard Eve's laughter.

I hit him harder.

I heard Erica giggling.

I hit him until something cracked.

Nate was still seated, but at that point he stood up and quietly walked out of the bar.

I never returned to the army. I never went back home, either. I made friends in all the wrong places. For six months after I deserted, I worked with all the people this world would be better without. I didn't have specific inclinations, I didn't get involved in the businesses; all I did was the killing. I spent four years acquiring certain skills and resources that I deemed necessary for what I had promised myself to do. By the time I was in that car on that road, I knew French, Russian and some German. I was excessively rich. By the time I was in that car, I had lost count of the people that had died by my hand.

159km/h

In the absence of Love, Violence had turned out to be a great mistress. At first I had rejected her, but she had grown on me. The most appealing thing about Violence, I had realized, was her simplicity: nothing can stop you when you want to hurt someone. The urge to destroy and how easily it can be satiated was almost unfair.

Violence is a shortcut, a facilitator. If you feel like a failure, she will give you the sense of success you yearn for. If you have desires unsatisfied, she will give you the chance to quench them. When I wanted to break something, I could do it and through Violence I reached pleasure, no matter how gluttonous. Violence was an easy way to overcome my frustration. For the weak, Violence is the answer. For me, it was a distraction. In overwhelming quantity, Violence allowed me to forget, but never forgive.

194km/h

"We declare that the splendor of the world has been enriched by a new beauty: the beauty of speed. A racing automobile with its bonnet adorned with great tubes like serpents of explosive breath—a roaring motor car which seems to run on machine-gun fire, is more beautiful than the Victory of Samothrace. We want to hymn the man at the wheel, who hurls the lance of his spirit across the Earth, along the circle of its orbit."

I had never understood that statement from the Futurist Manifesto until now. Now I felt it. I gripped the wheel tighter as the car grew harder to control. The speed was so entrancing; it allowed me, briefly, a gap, between all that I had become after I met Eve and that which I was intrinsically: heartbroken.

230km/h

The car hit the outer fence and ground against the mountain, breaking the glass of the passenger door. It wouldn't be much longer. For four years I had endured a lacerated spirit moved only by the hope of one day having again that which was mine and which was me. That day had come. What little I could see was blurred and I could hear nothing but the furious engine of the car. A curve, a bump, a hole would take me by surprise any second and it would all be over. Tears rolled on my cheeks and I screamed as I kicked the accelerator all the way it could go. I would see Erica again, in this life or the next.

I woke up relieved, rested, just like after a good night's sleep and you don't get the urge to stay in bed longer. It took me a bit to recall what had happened before I had blacked out, but then I saw it all again: the curve, the rail and the car rolling off the road. I moved my hand to my back. My gun was still there, tucked in my pants. Eve had said that she had no control of what people had on when she brought them over.

"Adam Lacroft," she said.

I jumped off the bed, pressed the gun against her forehead and slammed her against the wall. Her eyes widened in amazement and I saw the beginning of the smile that expressed her sick amusement at the things that I did that surprised her. She said something, but it was interrupted by the sound of the gunshot. A faint line of smoke emanated from the bullet hole in the wall, behind her intact head.

"Did that work out the way you planned it?"

"I knew nothing would happen. I just wanted you to see how serious I am when I say that, if I find a way, I will put a bullet in your head. Now that that's clear," I said as I tucked my gun back in my pants, "we can talk about why I'm here."

"The redhead," she said as she rolled her eyes.

I wrapped my hand around her throat. "Erica."

She laughed as she walked out of my hold, fading through my grip.

"My, my, how you've grown," she said as she sat in her chair. She crossed her legs seductively and gave me a wink. "Take a seat. I'm sure we can come to an *a*rrangement."

TO BE CONTINUED

Más Yo Que Yo Mismo

¡Oh vida mía, vida mía,
Agonice con tu agonía
Y con tu muerte me morí!
¡De tal manera te quería,
Que estar sin ti es estar sin mí!

¡Faro de mi devoción,
Perenne cual mi aflicción,
Es tu memoria bendita!
¡Dulce y santa lamparita
Dentro de mi corazón!

Luz que alumbra mi pesar,
Desde que tú te partiste
Y hasta el fin lo de alumbrar,
Que si me dejaste triste,
Triste me habrás de encontrar.

Y al abatir mi cabeza
Ya para siempre jamás,
El mal que a minarme empieza
Tú me reconocerás.

Merced al noble fulgor
Del recuerdo, mi dolor
Será espejo en que has de verte,
Y así vencerá a la muerte
La claridad del amor.

No habrá noche ni abismo
Que enflaquezca mi heroísmo
De buscarte sin cesar
Si eras más yo que yo mismo:
¡Cómo no te he de encontrar!

¡Oh vida mía, vida mía,
Agonice con tu agonía
Y con tu muerte me morí!
¡De tal manera te quería,
Que estar sin ti es estar sin mí!

La Amada Inmóvil—Amado Nervo, Febrero de 1912.

More Me Than Myself

Oh my life, my life,
I agonized with your agony
And I died with your death!
So much did I love you,
That to be without you is to be without me!

A beacon of my devotion,
Eternal as mi affliction,
Is your blessed memory!
Sweet and holy light
That rests in my heart!

Light that lights my gloom,
Since you last left me
And will continue to do so until the end,
For if you left me sad,
Sad you shall find me again.

And as I bow my head,
Now forever,
To the evil that starts to mine me,
I think because of my sadness
You will always recognize me.

Merciful is the noble brightness
Of memory, my pain
Will be the mirror in which you will always be
reflected,
And so will death be defeated
By the clarity of love.

There will be no night or abyss
That will weaken my heroism
Of searching for you non-stop.

If you were more me than myself:
How should I find you not!

Oh my life, my life,
I agonized with your agony
And I died with your death!
So much did I love you,
That to be without you is to be without me!

The Immovable Loved One—Amado Nervo, February,
1912 (Translated by me).

Thank-yous and shit

This is a work of fiction. Names, characters, places and incidents either are products of the author's imagination or are used fictitiously. Any resemblance to actual events or locales or persons, living or dead, is entirely coincidental. Except for you, Kaya Scodelario. I really do think you're the most gorgeous thing alive. If you ever read this, please go out with me. Cool.

The Godfather Death story is not of my imagination, it is a story created by the Grimm Brothers. It was very fitting, so thank you guys. I ask the reader that may find discrepancies between the army protocol in my story and the protocol in real life to fuck off. It's a book where Death is a hot, twenty-one-year-old, just let it go.

I want to thank my mom for her faith and for paying for everything. I want to thank my sister for finally getting off her fat ass and miraculously managing to read my book before it was published. I want to thank all the friends and family that have supported me from the beginning. I want to thank Professor Pedro Fuentes and Dr. Hector Hara, who both helped me with the medical issues treated in the novel. Dr Hara, sadly, died before I could show him the first manuscript. I hope Eve shows it to him and he approves the biological incongruence I might have invented with the information he gave me. I want to thank Rafael Casas and Carlos Ulloa who introduced me to Deborah Imershein, my editor. I want to thank Deborah for her patient and dedicated work and for helping turn this story into a respectable novel. (Hell, she even edited this thank-you note).

Finally, I want to thank you, for reading it. Truth be told, you, a complete stranger, are the most important component of my work and, hopefully, my career. Really, thank you for taking the time. I hope you liked

it. (If you did, tell a friend. If you didn't, tell an ex.)
Cheerio.